EMMA AND THE LEPRECHAUNS

EMMA AND THE LEPRECHAUNS

Elizabeth Daish

This first world edition published in Great Britain 2000 by
SEVERN HOUSE PUBLISHERS LTD of
9–15 High Street, Sutton, Surrey SM1 1DF.
This first world edition published in the USA 2000 by
SEVERN HOUSE PUBLISHERS INC of
595 Madison Avenue, New York, N.Y. 10022.

British Library Cataloguing in Publication Data

Daish,   Elizabeth
    Emma and the leprechauns
    1.   Sykes,   Emma   (Fictitious character) - Fiction
    I.   Title
    823.9'14 [F]

    ISBN 0-7278-5587-5

Typeset by Palimpsest Book Production Ltd.,
Polmont, Stirlingshire, Scotland.
Printed and bound in Great Britain by
MPG Books Ltd., Bodmin, Cornwall.

One

"You don't even look tired, sister." Eileen regarded Emma Sykes with an almost disappointed expression.

"We've been spoiled for so long that we were quite fit enough to face the plane journey home, and it was very comfortable." Emma laughed. "Having such a good housekeeper and seeing everything so immaculate helped, and I think I am quite unnecessary here and might go back to the States."

"Don't you dare! We've missed you something awful and Jean has been so excited that she will be playing with Rose again, you wouldn't believe."

Paul Sykes grinned and followed Mick into the office, noticing the air of confidence that showed how well Mick had reacted to the added responsibility of being in complete charge of the psychiatric clinic accounts and the general running of the establishment for so long while his employer lectured in America.

"I think you'll find everything OK, doc," Mick Grade said. "There were a few grumbles from some of your patients who wanted you and not a stranger to treat them, but most of them soon got used to Dr Forsyth and nobody really threw a wobbly. I promised the others

I'd book them in for appointments with you as soon as you felt like taking over, but most of the old lot needed help before you came back and you were away for so long that they finished their sessions with Dr Forsyth and liked him. The new ones have never met you. I've left a list of old patients who definitely want to see you, but I think it's more the fact that they like you as a person that makes them feel you're a friend. I've left the list on your desk and I'll get in touch with them when you're ready."

"Good thinking," Dr Sykes said approvingly. "I have to see some people today, but I can start a few sessions again in a day or so." He glanced in the desk diary. "Has it been as busy as this all the time we've been away?"

"No." Mick laughed. "Word got about among the medics that you were away and they hung back. There are a few fresh referrals now. They don't all know Dr Forsyth yet and they prefer you, but he's been a good locum and has been quite busy. Always cheerful and seems to enjoy it." Mick grinned. "Doesn't work as hard as you did because he didn't have the private patients to treat."

"He isn't here today?"

"Thought you'd like to nose around on your own first."

"Very tactful, but I shall be out for most of the afternoon."

"He said he'd be in for dinner tonight and, as my dear wife is besotted with him, that's no problem."

Paul laughed. "I gather that Eileen enjoyed being in charge as much as you did."

"Seventh heaven! Mind you, we missed you both. We all did. Mrs Coster was convinced that you would be killed by gangsters or little Rose would be kidnapped – but she's got a heart of gold really . . . sometimes." Mick shuffled some papers and looked cautious.

"Something wrong?" asked Paul.

"Not really. It's just Mrs Coster's daughter, Maureen. She really is good with kiddies and liked it when we said she could babysit and help out when Eileen was busy, but she wants to be a regular nanny and keeps on about it. Mrs Coster isn't much help as that's what she wants her to do. We can't afford a nanny for Jean and it wouldn't be fair to you and Emma to have you pay for one for both Jean and Rose."

"I'll leave that to my wife to settle, but Maureen might as well stay on to babysit and make herself generally useful on a part-time basis."

Mick looked relieved. "If we had another baby . . . or you and Emma had another, there's no doubt she'd be very useful."

Paul raised an enquiring eyebrow but Mick shook his head. "Nothing to report on that angle. Eileen made the excuse that she couldn't be pregnant while you were away, but you are back now and I'll have a few words with her. Jean needs a brother or sister."

The two men exchanged serious glances. "You'd love Bea's three youngsters now that they're growing up," said Paul. "I hoped it might make Emma broody, but we mere men have to wait and see."

"Tea and scones for now," Eileen said, coming in and putting a tray on the desk. "There's a nice shoulder of lamb for tonight. Dr Forsyth used to give me all his meat coupons and hardly ever ate his share here, so I saved them for a real joint when he brought Sister Bright over for an evening, and I still think in that way." She laughed. "I can't get used to rationing being over at last and meat being the last to come off coupons, but I've kept my ration books, to show Jean when she grows up just what we had to put up with for all these years. But there are still shortages, and I buy what I see when I can and put it in the fridge. It's got to be such a habit that I carry a newspaper in my bag in case I see something I can buy that needs wrapping up!"

Emma poured tea and sighed. "There's a lot that we shall miss that we had in America. It's wicked what there is so freely available over there; people waste a lot of good food. Who would believe that we still queued for the basic provisions so long after the end of the war? Maybe next year, in 1957, we shall be able to forget the hard times."

"We were better off than most," Eileen said.

"Is Sister Bright coming tonight?" Emma asked, and Eileen giggled.

"They hit it off right from that night you had them to dinner to see if Dr Forsyth was suitable as a locum. They see a lot of each other now and I thought you'd like to see her."

"No ring?"

"Not yet, but they are very keen." Eileen nodded wisely. "You can tell at a glance."

Emma stretched. "I ought to drag the girls away from Mrs Coster and unpack Rose's case. I gave Rose the presents for Mrs Coster and one for Maureen and I left them oohing and aahing over them. It seemed a good idea at the time when we bought them, but now I wonder if six pairs of coloured stockings will suit Maureen. She does have rather fat legs." She wrinkled her nose. "My mind went blank when I tried to choose something for Mrs Coster but Bea said she'd want something useful. We bought a pile of very nice bright pinafores and one really frilly one for fun."

Mick laughed. "She'll be wearing one as soon as she sees them. Don't be surprised if she spends tomorrow brushing the front steps so that the cleaner next door will see and admire."

Emma glanced back from the doorway to the warm and comfortable room and decided how good it was to be back home again. What now? she thought as she ran down the broad stairway. The idea of hard work was oddly satisfying, and she looked forward to meeting Robert Forsyth again; but she had decided while she was away that she must make sure she did less on the housekeeping side as Eileen was now officially the housekeeper and thriving on the responsibility.

There would be time to take Rose to visit friends, and she'd have free time for herself, unless . . . Unless she had another child. Her pulse quickened. It was possible. She felt a mixture of hope and dread and turned her thoughts away to the two little girls "helping" Mrs Coster to dust the banister rails.

Two floral blouses and a folding silk umbrella for

Eileen were in the main suitcase, and Emma partly unpacked enough of Paul's cases to find the leather jacket that they'd bought for Mick.

"It's better than Christmas," Eileen said as she held one of the blouses up in front of her dark dress. "No, Jean, you mustn't open the umbrella indoors. It's bad luck!"

"I bought one for Jean, too." Emma handed over the small umbrella and a matching rain cape and hood. "Rose loves hers and we used them twice in the States." She went back to the bedroom, suddenly unsure of what to do. Ridiculous! she thought. I'm home again and should be in charge, but I feel like a visitor. Paul was meeting colleagues in St Thomas's and Eileen was preparing dinner and obviously needed no help in the kitchen. Rose came into the bedroom and sat on the stool by the dressing table, dangling her short legs and looking into the mirror with an expression that showed she was not happy. "What is it, darling?"

"I want Mark," she said, and a tear escaped and rolled down her cheek.

"I know." Emma hugged her and the two faces reflected in the glass had the same expression. "Tomorrow we'll go and see Peter Pan in the park and buy ice cream."

"Pistachio? That's my favourite."

"I doubt if they sell it here. I remember vanilla and strawberry and sometimes chocolate, but I've not tasted pistachio in London."

"Mark likes strawberry," Rose said. "Why didn't he come back with us?"

6

Emma sighed and for the third time explained that Auntie Bea couldn't spare any of her three children and Mark, the youngest, wouldn't want to leave his family. "When I ring Bea, you shall speak to him."

"I'll be in bed," grumbled Rose.

"If you're awake I'll bring you down to the phone," Emma promised, and saw that the long journey was catching up on the little girl. "Bath and bed early, and maybe you'll wake up in time to talk to Mark."

The house was peaceful. Rose and Jean were asleep, worn out by the excitement, and Emma set up a drinks tray in the drawing room ready to receive Dr Forsyth and Sister Joan Bright.

Mick stood in the doorway and smiled. "It's great to have you back, and everything must be as it was. Don't think you have to ask us to your dinner parties and social things. We don't have them and we have our own flat and a life of our own downstairs. I believe in a bit of space out of working hours," he said bluntly.

"What a wise creature you are, Mick, but you'll have a welcome-home drink with us, won't you?"

"Sure. Business as usual tomorrow?"

"Yes, business as usual, but Paul and I were talking about you on the plane and decided that you and Eileen will need a holiday after all the responsibility we left for you. Any ideas? My Aunt Emily on the Island has said often enough that you're welcome to use my cottage there at any time, but perhaps there are other places that might appeal more?"

Mick sighed. "Eileen wants to go there, but if I can twist her arm I'd like to go to Ireland."

7

"Of course, you are half Irish and must have family there."

"Not really. Maybe an old aunt or two, but we've never kept in touch and I shan't visit them. I haven't been there for years but I like the people and I think Jean would have a good time. They like kiddies over there."

Emma heard the front doorbell and hurried to meet her guests, but said to Mick as she left the room, "Make any arrangements you like and we'll fit them in. Do it soon – you both deserve a rest and a change."

Joan Bright looked pretty and had the kind of expression that hinted at a deep contentment. She hugged Emma and Robert Forsyth grinned and kissed Emma's cheek. "It's good to see you again," he said.

"Paul and I have so much to thank you for, Robert. I doubt if he would have been able to concentrate on his work in the States without knowing that you were here in charge of his patients." Emma's eyes twinkled. "Not that you look worn out. I think this place suits you . . . or something does. And nobody would think that Joan was a hard-working casualty sister."

Joan blushed and removed her left glove. The ring sparkled under the hall light and Emma caught her breath. "We decided yesterday before you came back, as we have to plan our future, together if possible."

Robert looked serious. "When this job ends I could go anywhere, and I can't leave Joan at Beattie's and risk losing her."

"Let's have a drink to celebrate your engagement," Paul said, and Emma realised that he had been listening from the stairs. "Wonderful news," he added warmly and led the way to the drawing room. "Drinks now and dinner while we bore you with talk of America, and shop-talk about work here can wait until coffee-time."

"I should have rung Aunt Emily," Emma said.

"As you'll need at least an hour, leave it until tomorrow," Paul said drily. "Better still, pack a bag and visit her for a few days. Rose is upset at leaving her friends and Aunt Emily is good for her."

"I can't go now," Emma began.

"Why not? Cheers," Paul said dismissively. "Have some of these Yankee crisps. Not as good as ours but not bad."

"Do they come with a twist of blue paper of salt in each packet, like ours?" asked Robert.

"Nothing so sophisticated. All neat and tidy in a box, but almost too salty. However, can't look a gift horse as they say, and we can go back to Smith's crisps next week."

Emma felt nostalgic as the meal progressed and the picture of life with Bea, Dwight and the children unfolded. Paul said little about the work there until coffee was being poured, then eyed Robert speculatively. "Have you decided what you'd like to do?" he asked.

Robert shrugged. "I've had two offers, one from Wales and one from Canada, which would mean a fairly traumatic break for a number of years." He glanced at Joan, who sat very still but looked pale. "It's a good offer but we both prefer to stay in England and Joan wants to go on working."

9

"Tell me, did you really enjoy working here?"

"It was marvellous, and I had the feeling that I was doing some good with at least five patients who really need long-term therapy."

"And you hate the idea of handing them over to me?"

Robert looked embarrassed. "It's not that." He grinned. "I don't think so. But in a way you're right. They trust me."

"Then why not continue with the treatment?" Paul said casually.

"What do you mean? If I take another job that will be impossible."

"Not if you stay here and work with me."

"But I can't do that . . . can I?"

"I asked Mick to give me a run-down about expenses and bookings and a lot that I had no idea we'd need to study about the private patients. I asked Dr Shilton to take over while I was away, as I wanted a salaried locum here to deal with just the National Health patients. I couldn't expect my private patients to accept a new man who wasn't a recognised consultant. In any case, it would have overloaded you, as it has me at times."

"I had noticed," Emma said with feeling.

"Mick is wonderful. He works hard and has a fund of common sense that outweighs any lack of formal education. He says very firmly that I need and can afford a partner. One man can't be on call all the time and everyone needs regular breaks covered by someone who really knows about the clinics." Paul smiled. "I heard quite a lot about you today, Robert.

Shilton handed me back my patients and suggested you were ready to take some of them, as he'd heard how well you managed the National Health list."

Robert's voice was unsteady. "Do you mean you want me to stay on a permanent basis?"

"I'm offering you a junior partnership unless you have other plans."

Joan Bright sank her head on to her hands and gave a strangled sob. When she looked up her eyes were full of tears. "What a wonderful engagement present," she said.

"That's a relief," Paul said lightly to break the tension. "I couldn't go through all that fuss, interviewing suitable and unsuitable candidates again."

"I'll keep the flat in Covent Garden and use the rooms I've had here while you were away, if that's OK?"

"We'll discuss what alterations we'll need to make another spare room into a second consulting room tomorrow. It will be a relief to get you settled: I may have more lectures to give and that will leave the bulk of the work with you for a while," Paul said apologetically.

"Fine. I want to earn my keep!"

"More lectures?" Emma asked.

"Some I can do alone if they take only a weekend, but others might be longer and you'll have to hold my hand. You know how I loathe lonely hotel rooms," Paul said.

"Not yet I hope," Emma said with feeling. "We've just arrived back and I have a hundred things to do and people to visit."

"Times change," said Robert. "Paul has so many contacts now and is important in the profession."

"It cuts both ways," Paul replied. "I have prestige and work I enjoy, but increasingly there will be times when I don't treat patients, but just talk about how it should be done."

"The price of fame," Robert said drily. "Maybe some day I should be so lucky! But lectures are important and the next generation of psychiatrists will need you, Paul."

"I do seem to have achieved a reputation for the treatment of battle fatigue and the functional disorders caused by trauma," Paul admitted. "But I enjoy the hands-on, one-to-one situation between doctor and patient and would hate to miss that. I think one's sensitivity could become blunted by all the theory and no human contact."

Joan sighed. "I know what you mean, Paul. We find the same thing happening in nursing. If a nurse is good, she has promotion to ward-sister status or in one of the departments such as theatre or my department, casualty, but we either find that we are indispensable in that category and stay on that salary or we are shunted up to an admin post where we lose touch with the everyday life of a department." Her laugh was without humour. "Often the ones who are not very efficient as working sisters are given admin jobs with increased salaries just to get them out of the way of doing something harmful on the practical side. I can think of at least two who should not be in charge of a busy ward, so they have been promoted out of harm's way, and now they swan about looking very important."

"You know you'd hate that," Robert said firmly. "I heard on the grapevine that you'd refused to be home sister."

"Who told you that?" Joan looked indignant and then smiled. "Can you imagine me checking rooms for new nurses, making sure they come in before midnight and all the silly things to do with linen and laundry?"

"I believe you'd soon be out of a job if you were home sister," Emma said. "I hear that soon such jobs will be done by what amount to civil servants with no hospital background at all."

"As it hardly affects the patients, I can see why it would free real nurses for more important work; and if they allow nurses to live outside the nurses' home and have private lives of their own it will be impossible to impose all the silly rules that have tied nurses in training for so long." Joan laughed. "Until they open that door, I'd better get back to my chaste room in hospital! I'm on duty tomorrow morning, so we'd better go now, if Robert is ready."

Two

E mma sounded the motor horn and Rose tried to open the car door as Emily Dewar walked down the garden path to the gate. "Are you sure you want us in the house? We can go to the cottage," Emma suggested.

"I'll see more of you here. If Rose is in bed, you'll be tied, so park that thing over there and bring in your bags. I've got the kettle on the boil."

"When wasn't a kettle ready for tea in this house?" Emma released the door latch and Rose flung herself towards her great-aunt Emily.

"Steady! You've grown so much you'll have me over," Emily said with barely hidden delight. "Come in and get your coat off and tell me all about America." Emily accepted Rose's hugs but made no attempt to embrace her niece. Emma smiled, knowing how much this visit meant to the elderly spinster aunt who had been more than a mother to her all her life. Outward signs of affection had never been Emily's way, but the love she felt for Emma and now Rose was there as she said, "You look well, I must say."

Rose carried her own small case and put it in the large cot that Emily kept for her use and had used for Clive, Rose's cousin, when he was small enough to fit into it.

Emily looked amused. "You're staying then?"

"Yes, and I want to see the chickens next door."

"Play with your Noah's Ark while Aunt Emily and I have a cup of tea and then we'll walk to the farm and buy some eggs, if we need any."

Emily added a generous tot of whiskey to her own cup and handed Emma a less lethal brew of weaker tea and milk. "Now tell me how Bea is, and the children." Emily's dark brown eyes glowed both anticipation and for the next half an hour Emma recounted details that she knew she'd want to hear, the amusing episodes and the less pleasant details of the time when they'd thought that Mark had been lost or stolen – but he'd been found hiding in the trunk of Dwight's car.

"And little Rose sat on a pony?"

"She loved it."

"My father would have liked that. He was a fine horseman and tried to make us all take to the saddle, but we were no good at it."

"Bea sent her love and hopes to see you soon if Dwight can spare the time. He may have to come over on official duty so keep your fingers crossed."

"They can't come for another month or so but I shall see them again when they come to London."

Emma laughed. "I might have known that *you* could tell *me* that. You were also right when you said we must watch Mark, and to warn Bea that someone was stealing her trinkets. Dwight now regards you as his personal oracle and he wants to know when you're going over to sort out the White House!"

"Silly monkey!" Emily said but blushed slightly.

"Now for *your* news."

"Not a lot to tell. You know that George and Margaret were married soon after you left for the States." Emma nodded. "Nice wedding. His mother was shedding a few tears of happiness. Janey always was a bit like that, but it was a relief to her that George seemed to have got over his crush on you."

"It could never have been possible," Emma said firmly. "First cousins, and other things like the fact that I love Paul. Now that I have Rose and George has Clive from his first marriage, any closer relationship between us gets ever more remote. He does love Margaret. He said so. They have a lot in common and they're good together. The fact that they have both suffered helps to give them mutual sympathy."

Emily gave her an old-fashioned look. "Just as well you were in America and stayed away long enough for them to get their bearings."

"That's ridiculous. He's . . . cured, and they'll be very happy." Defiantly, Emma looked at her aunt. "When we're settled I intend inviting them to stay. Paul thinks it's a good idea and I want to get to know Margaret. I've met her only once or twice and I like what I saw."

"Give it a few weeks." Emily's gaze on the glowing fire that she kept alight winter and summer was steady and absorbed, as if she saw visions in the caverns of red coals. "George is happy, but she needs time."

"What do you mean?"

"She lost her first love at sea and she needs George to be completely hers. Inside, she's frightened of losing him, not by death this time, but to another woman."

"But she knows he meets many attractive women in the Admiralty and onshore bases, and they mean nothing to him. They chose each other, Aunt Emily, and they had enough faith to be married!"

"Not just any other woman, Emma. You."

"I can't listen to this. When I saw George here before we went to the States, he was calm and friendly but that's all. He will remember me with affection, family affection, but that's all."

Emily looked at Emma's flushed face. "I agree that you have nothing to fear from George, but you can't avoid the fact that he was in love with you and there will always be a trace of that left whatever happens. In her mind, Margaret might believe he still hankers after what she imagines might have been."

"Sometimes you talk rubbish, Emily Dewar," Emma said. "It's time I fetched the eggs with Rose, before she goes to bed. Anything else you need from the farm?"

"Take the small basket for Rose and let her find the eggs. Take your time: the casserole will be fine in the oven for another hour. Rose can have a fresh boiled egg with toast when you come back."

"It really will be all right," Emma said, as if to convince herself, but she needed reassurance.

"It will be when she is expecting, but she may need help."

"Soon?"

17

"Soon enough. Now put Rose's coat on. It's turning chilly."

Rose ran on ahead, waving her small willow basket, and looked under the hedge where she knew some hens laid eggs away from their pens. She shouted and an irate hen clucked and flew out from the hedge, leaving an egg that Rose pounced on with glee.

Emma left her to search again and walked slowly up to the farmhouse. She was troubled. George was a friend and nothing more. Well . . . maybe a little more than that – a cousin for whom she had great affection – and she was proud of his achievements in the Navy. He was a good son to Aunt Janey, Emily's sister, and a loving father to Clive, the boy born to Sadie, George's American wife, not long before she died of meningitis.

She pulled at a long grass and plucked off the feathery top, sending a cloud of small seeds into the breeze. The green stem was crisp between her teeth and reminded her of picnics on the Downs near Tennyson's monument, and Philip, the boy who had wanted her from their schooldays.

Don't be stupid, she told herself. Aunt Emily is too fey at times and she sees what she thinks she wants to see. George and Margaret have been married for such a short time that any undercurrent of doubt has not had time to show, if indeed it exists, and yet . . . Thinking of Philip, she knew that she had never felt anything more than a sibling affection for him, and the pleasant *frisson* of sexuality between two young people thrown together by school contacts and sport.

She had been relieved when the handsome Air Force officer he became had gone to live and be married in South Africa.

George was different, she admitted. He was family and as such had a warmer place in her heart, and they shared a similar sense of humour, but he was no longer in love with her and she couldn't imagine him giving his new bride cause for concern.

"Emma! Your aunt told me you'd be here today." Meg Caws smiled and took the basket that Rose held up. "Four eggs? You have been busy," she said. "Come in while I make it the dozen and take some butter, too."

The old dairy was light and cool. Eggs were stacked ready for sale in cardboard trays while damp butter-muslin was draped over pats of butter carefully weighed into half-pound slabs so recently that beads of whey still clung to the pats. "Can you spare the butter?" Emma asked.

"We've more than enough for the shop, and rationing never was more than a joke with us. I used to make pats like this to a given weight in case the inspectors came nosing around, but I made some the old way to please the people up at the manor and did some in moulds like my granny used to do." She smiled down at Rose. "I've made one for you. Do you want the sheaf of corn or the cow's face, my love?"

"The cow." Rose gazed at the round slab of butter with the face of a smiling cow moulded on the surface. "May I keep it?"

"Only until you get home, then Auntie will put it in

her fridge and you can have some bread and butter with your boiled egg."

"It's too nice to cut up!"

"The weather's too warm to keep it out of a fridge and it would melt if you tried to play with it." Meg saw that Rose was about to rebel and changed the subject. "What was your favourite thing that you did in America? You are a very lucky little girl. I've never been in a great big ship like the *Queen Mary.*"

Rose prattled on about Mark and the ponies, and Mark, and Mark, until Emma tried to keep him out of the conversation. "We must go back. Aunt Emily will think we're lost. Thank you, Meg. Aunt Emily said to put the eggs and butter on her bill, and she'd like another dozen eggs the day after tomorrow as she wants to make cakes."

Emma walked along the lane by the farm and stopped to unlock the door of her cottage. She glanced in each room to make sure there was nothing urgent needed there. Wilf, the handyman, had left fires laid, and the stove and windows shone. If Mick and Eileen chose the island for their break, the cottage would be neat and tidy and welcoming, but when she took Rose back to Aunt Emily, boiled eggs and fresh bread and butter she wondered if they would use the cottage or go to Ireland instead.

"Have you ever been to Ireland?" she asked when Rose was in bed and Emily was serving the rabbit and dumpling casserole.

Emily paused with the serving spoon over the dish.

She gave the rabbit a prod and ladled joints out on to plates. "What brought that on? You aren't thinking of going, are you?"

"No," Emma said slowly. "At least I had never really considered it, but Mick has his heart set on going there and it did remind me that you are half Irish; and from what I hear the country is very beautiful."

Emily frowned. "None of us went there. My mother left her family when she married my father and pride made her stay away as they didn't approve of her marrying an English soldier and she was a lapsed Catholic." Emily thought for a moment. "She talked enough about the green fields and the goats and donkeys on the hills, the wonderful fishing and the lilting music played in pubs and at family gatherings, but she never would tell us about her parents and friends. Your grandfather didn't encourage talk of Ireland, and she was a peace keeper, so she kept her thoughts to herself."

"It must have been hard to leave all that behind and come to live in a strange land."

"There were times when I thought she needed to cry, but for all her sweetness she was a strong woman. You have her picture, Emma, and in many ways I see her in you."

"I'm glad. Maybe one day I'll go there and try to find something or someone with memories of people close to her."

"Eat up before it gets cold," Emily said briskly. "You wouldn't know where to start looking, and she was there so long ago that nobody will be alive who knew her. I never asked the name of her village or town.

They all seem to be called Ballysomething and meant nothing to us. We were heedless children and it never seemed important. She belonged with us and that's all we needed to know. Ireland was a foreign country and none of us wanted to kiss the Blarney Stone." She chuckled. "Mother did say that my brother Jack must have kissed it as he was so full of himself and never at a loss for words."

"Isn't it strange that when someone or a place is mentioned by a friend or in the newspaper, the same name crops up again and again? Since Mick mentioned Ireland, I've read two articles about it; one on the Ring of Kerry and one on the Mountains of Mourne. They sound so romantic, and a patient of Paul's who is Irish talked about his boyhood there, when he was under hypnosis."

"Did he give Mick the idea of going there?"

Emma's eyes widened. "I think you may be right. It wasn't a visit to Ireland that he wanted to describe to Robert when Mick was in the consulting room, but affectionate references to what must have been a very relaxed and happy childhood. His psychiatric trouble began later, in the war." She laughed. "He's very well off and tried to persuade Mick to leave us and go with him to his stately home over there to act as chauffeur, valet and general dogsbody, but Mick laughed it off. He said he liked the old smoke, and had a wife and child to keep him here, and his work with us was more important than being a general skivvy in Ireland, however well paid it would be!"

"But what he said must have made an impression on Mick."

"Enough to make him want to see where he had his roots. I know from experience of patients that Irishmen have a lot of charm and the ability to describe places and people very well."

"Mother used to say that some of them could charm the birds from the trees if they had a mind to do so." Emily shook her head. "She chose your grandfather. He had charm when he wanted something, and he was a hard man who knew what he wanted."

Emma helped herself to more mashed potato. "Some of the things you cook are Irish. There's plenty of potato left, so can we have colcannon tomorrow? It's one way to make Rose eat cabbage when it's mixed with mash and butter."

Emily lit an oil lamp as day merged with twilight and set it on the faded chenille tablecloth. Emma felt cosseted as they sat and drank more tea, and talked or were silent, in perfect contentment.

Emma glanced at her aunt's face, thinner than she recalled it from childhood but still strong and kind. The soft lamplight and the dying fire made shadows and wove dreams, and Emily seemed more Irish than usual as she sat with a small piece of crochetwork turning between her fingers. Emma suppressed a yawn. "It's been a full day," she said. "I'll get the present I brought from America and the parcel that Bea wanted you to have. Her father packed what she ordered, so it's really from Switzerland and not from the States. Bea knew you'd prefer the real thing as you don't care for American biscuits."

Emily gloated over the sealed tin of Swiss chocolate

biscuits and the slabs of milk chocolate. "Bea knows I like a nice biscuit," she said with satisfaction. "I shall keep these for when I'm alone or when Janey comes to stay. I'm not wasting them on Rose or you!"

"Very wise. I wondered if your feet were still troubling you? These might help in the house."

Emily slipped into the soft leather moccasins and regarded her feet with amusement. "As Mother would say, 'They're grand, just grand.'" She smoothed the line of coloured beads that decorated the fronts and the slender thong that adjusted the fit.

"They're real Indian moccasins; you can wear them out of doors as well as in the house. They're strongly made, of real deerskin."

"I shall wear them in the house. I may have dark hair and eyes but I'm not a squaw."

Emma heard her chuckling as she climbed the stairs to bed, and was soon asleep, hardly hearing the country sounds of the night.

Three

"We took you at your word, sister, but I wonder if it isn't a bit too soon."

"You both need a holiday, and I'm glad you chose Ireland. The North sounds a bit risky just now but you should be fine in the countryside of southern Ireland." Emma regarded Mick with interest. "You look Irish enough to pass for a local and Jean has the creamy skin and slightly auburn hair that shows her heritage."

"Don't worry about us, sister. There've been troubles in Ireland since Cromwell's time and I shall agree with every political opinion I hear over there. I managed to get on with Jocks and Pats in the Army and never had any trouble." He grinned. "You know me, a born coward."

"That isn't true! Sometimes I wish he was a bit more placid," Eileen said. "But he does get on with most people and gets his own way most of the time." She sighed. "I'm looking forward to it, but I hope it doesn't leave too much for you to do, sister, now that Dr Paul's clinic will be busy and he'll need you in there for most of the time." Eileen poured coffee and handed round the home-made cakes, making sure that the two little girls had plates to gather their crumbs.

25

"Maureen can take Rose out for walks while I'm in the clinic, and Sister Bright has some unused holiday that she's taking to settle their rooms here to her satisfaction, and she'll help in Robert's clinic too."

"Everything seems to be organised," Eileen admitted. "I wish it was like that everywhere. I hate to read the papers, and Mrs Coster gets very upset at some of the things she reads and takes as gospel truth. She was almost in tears about Princess Margaret."

"Something I missed?"

"They said she was being forced to give up that nice Group Captain Townsend. If ever there was a love story, that's it, and yet they aren't going to be allowed to marry as he's divorced!" Eileen sniffed. "The Archbishop and the Prime Minister both had a go at the poor girl and I think they'll send him off to a faraway place so they can't meet again."

"Nice-looking couple," Mick said. "But there's plenty of unmarried men she can have, and some have wealth and a title into the bargain."

"Are you suggesting she would want anyone else, Mick Grade? What if I'd been told not to marry you, would just any man have done for me? She ought to fight for him, or so Mrs Coster says."

"Surely she wasn't crying over *them*? That's old news. I found her in tears but then I had to answer the phone and couldn't find out why she was upset." Emma looked worried. "It must have been something more."

"She went to the market and saw her son who runs a stall there."

"One of her grandchildren isn't ill? They seem to

have charmed lives, in spite of their surroundings and living conditions. It must be impossible to keep rooms clean with all that smoke from the laundry chimneys next door."

"Sid was telling her that since Ruth Ellis was hung for murder, there have been rows in Parliament and the lawyers are having a fine old time as usual."

"When I heard that she was condemned I never thought they'd hang a woman. That went out years ago and most cases of murder have life imprisonment." Emma felt cold. She had seen photographs of the pretty young woman and suddenly the thought of that slender neck being subjected to the hangman's rope was frightening. What must the hangman have thought? she wondered. Could he forget his day's work and go home satisfied? "Mrs Coster reads all the newspapers that carry lurid articles and horrible pictures and seems to enjoy them, so why did this affect her so much? I know it's been in the papers for months and everyone seems to have his or her own ideas about capital punishment, but it's hardly news any more."

"Sid said that all tarts should be shot, not hanged like Ruth Ellis. He said she killed her lover in cold blood and hanging was too good for her! I think Mrs Coster is more upset about her son than about the hanging of a murderess. It's more personal than that." Mick put his empty coffee cup on the tray.

"Why?"

"Sid's girl jilted him and he's seen her about with another man, so he's very bitter. Mrs Coster thinks there'll be a punch-up," Mick said calmly. "If there is it's best to get it over somewhere quiet, but she thinks he'll do Maisie's new boyfriend a real injury. Sid's a big lad and he's been in trouble before, for a fight in the Mason's Arms last year."

"Mrs Coster talked to me about Maisie and said how much she liked her. She hoped it would make Sid more reasonable as she had a good influence over him. If they have parted, I know that Mrs Coster will be very upset," Emma said. "She might worry in case Sid hurts Maisie as well as her new boyfriend."

"Sid's a wide-boy with too much to say for himself," Mick said. "He means no harm until he drinks, then his fists talk louder than words. He dresses like a teddy boy and mixes with some very odd people. Most of the teds are OK but some carry bicycle chains and flick-knives, and I wonder if Sid is one of them."

"No wonder his mother is frightened," Emma said. "I must have a chat with her."

"I think he imagines strange things, like a man has DTs when he drinks too much. He swore he saw a flying saucer last week and started a fight with a man who said they were a hoax and didn't exist, but Sid swore that he's seen one like the ones they're seeing over Warminster."

Eileen sniffed. "He saw it in the bottom of a beer glass, I expect."

"A lot of people say they've seen them, and a man told the papers that he saw strange men peering at him from one that came down low."

Paul grinned. "I can't wait for someone to tell me all

about how he met little green men. That will happen one day, under hypnosis. It's bound to happen!"

"What if there *are* people living on another planet in outer space? It isn't impossible, is it?" Emma asked.

"Best ask your Aunt Emily. She's the one who knows what goes on everywhere!"

"No, Mick. I can't think of her talking to aliens from another world. She's far too busy sorting out her own friends and relatives."

"Any news that we should hear?" asked Paul with amusement.

"Nothing that isn't private," Emma replied with dignity.

Eileen looked anxious. "Nothing bad, I hope."

"Nothing that can't be put right for us, and she thinks you'll enjoy Ireland."

"I told you it would be all right," Mick said triumphantly. "If Miss Dewar says we'll be OK that's enough for me." He glanced at the clock on the wall and hurried out of the office and Eileen took the two girls along to the nursery. Paul turned to Emma.

"We haven't had time to talk since you came back. Did Emily say something that wasn't what you wanted to hear?"

Emma moved restlessly and fiddled with a pen that lay on the desk. "Nothing specific, but she is concerned about Margaret, George's new wife."

He nodded. "Go on."

"You aren't surprised?"

"Not really. George will never be free of you, Emma. Can't say I blame him," he added and smoothed her hair away from her troubled face. "Let's invite them to stay

29

and make sure she's convinced she's the only important lady in his life."

"You've planned something?"

"I've told Robert about them and he agrees that she may need help."

"Aunt Emily said she'd need help but I thought it might be when she's pregnant, not that she'd need a psychiatrist."

"When she's here Robert will speak to her if she needs someone. I'm too close and he can be objective. I think he could be very helpful."

"It might be tricky. If she thinks we want to help in that way she may jump to the conclusion that we think she's crazy, or that I'm trying to hide something."

"If she talks to Robert, who she's never met, it will be in order for him to ask casual questions about her past and what she wants to do in the future. We keep quiet and just make sure she has a good time in London. What does she like? Concerts, rock and roll, shopping?"

Emma giggled. "We can try all three, but I don't think she's the type for 'Rock around the Clock'."

"You never know. Even cool-looking blondes like Bea have been known to do it."

"Bea has to be half American now, at least on the surface, and she always did enjoy dancing."

"Do you think we should lend Mick a car for Ireland? I mentioned it, but he seemed a bit unwilling to take it."

"Some people have had damage done to cars with English numberplates, so it might be wiser if they hire a car when they reach Dublin."

"At least we can drive them to the station and see them off. Why the pensive face?" He kissed her. "They'll be fine, and you'll be too busy to miss them."

"It's not that. In a way I envy them. I talked with Aunt Emily about Ireland and I believe I'd like to go there one day."

"We might have to do that anyway. I have invitations to lecture in Dublin and Belfast, and they would like me to go there soon."

"Why the urgency?"

Paul shrugged. "I seem to be the one they want as they have so many soldiers and civilians caught up in the troubles. There's a lot of battle fatigue." Paul looked thoughtful. "I met a doctor who was on leave from the Army after being stationed in Belfast. He hates his work there after seeing more torn limbs and wasted lives than he knew existed. I think he needs help as much as some of his patients, but as he's a surgeon and not a shrink he fails to recognise his own need."

"If Mick and Eileen leave in five days' time, we could be ready for visitors the next weekend, if George can get leave."

"Try your Aunt Janey. She knows what they do and when they're free as they go to her often to see Clive."

"Did you get through?" asked Paul later.

"She's going to hear from George tonight, so I left it with her to arrange something. That may be her now, but you'd better answer it as it might be for you."

Emma sat on the edge of the desk and eyed her

husband with curiosity. The Paul she knew sounded quite different from the Dr Sykes who spoke about patients and his work on the phone, but he was smiling as he handed the receiver to Emma.

"Aunt Janey? Yes, we had a wonderful time." At least five minutes passed before Janey was convinced that her niece had returned from the terrors of Washington in one piece, but at last Emma asked if she thought that George and his wife would be able to visit them.

"They're both at the Admiralty place in Bath," Janey said. "It's been wonderful for them, as George could easily have been in Scotland and Margaret in Portsmouth."

"So you think they'll come to stay for a few days when they have leave?"

"It would fit in very well. I want to go over to see Emily, and if they can bring Clive to you it would be a change all round." She hesitated.

"Something wrong, Aunt Janey?"

"No. George is having leave almost at once, as if he might be sent away, and as this awful business about the Suez Canal is getting out of hand, a warship might be sent there to look after British interests. George says that Colonel Nasser intends to nationalise the canal and throw out all foreign pilots and personnel."

"I thought the pilots taking liners through the canal had to be very skilled. Surely they can't let untrained men take over?"

"George says that we underestimate the Egyptians. After all, they have sailed the world for hundreds of years, just as we have, and a lot of Egyptian sailors and soldiers have trained at Dartmouth and Sandhurst and done well."

"Margaret must be worried in case there's a conflict when George is there. I hope they agree to come to us. I want to get to know her well, and if Clive comes too Rose will be very excited."

"Clive might help a lot," Janey said drily. "Nothing like a couple of noisy children to take Margaret's mind off her own doubts."

"You've been talking to Aunt Emily," Emma accused her.

"I have eyes too! Margaret is happy in many ways but George is as attractive as his father was and she's afraid of losing him." She sounded wistful. "I see my first husband every time George is here."

"George doesn't want other women, just as your husband wanted only you. When you were widowed and then married his best friend, Alex, it may have been second best but you are very happy. It's quite obvious that you have a good marriage, and a bond because of Clive."

"Yes, I'm happy, and I worry too much. I hope you're right, Emma. I know George doesn't run after other women but you were the first love of his life, before Sadie and before Margaret, and this meeting will be important to both George and Margaret."

"George and I are cousins and could never be more than that," Emma reminded her firmly. "If you can arrange to have Clive brought here or to George, and let us know when they'll arrive, we can do the rest."

33

Elizabeth Daish

"Do you think they'll come?" asked Paul after Emma
had replaced the receiver.

"Aunt Janey seemed almost certain, and once they
mention it to Clive I know they'll have no peace until
he comes to London. He missed the Changing of the
Guard at Buckingham Palace when he came here last
and we must make sure he sees it this time."

"You seem pleased."

"There's no reason why I shouldn't be," Emma said
shortly. "They are family, and Rose adores Clive." She
smiled. "You do like George, don't you?"

"Very much, but I feel for him if he has two lovely
ladies to tug at his heartstrings! Maybe I shall flirt with
Margaret."

"You aren't the flirty type," Emma said with satisfaction. "And you wouldn't dare!" She looked at the
rolled-up map on the desk. "Have you lost Europe?"
she asked.

"Mick was looking at the map of the world and trying
to seem unconcerned, and I doubt if geography is his
favourite subject, but I think he's worried about the
international situation. If our troops become involved
with another country, he's still young enough to be
called up, even if he was given a complete discharge
and isn't even in the reserve."

"Why is he worried?"

"Suez is important, as George knows. Nasser was
furious when Britain and America refused to pay for
the new Aswan Dam in Egypt and has turned to Russia
for help. To show his independence he's threatening to
sink several ships to block the canal and says that we

34

now have no claim on the canal and its future revenues. If ships can't use it, they will have to sail an extra six thousand miles round Africa to get to the Red Sea from the Mediterranean, which could involve our navy."

"That shouldn't affect Mick. He isn't a sailor."

"That's not the only trouble spot. He's been a soldier and he thinks that the situation in Hungary is dangerous too. From Mick's point of view the Hungarian uprising could bring our army into their conflict with Russia."

Emma looked worried. "So George might be sent to Suez, and United Nations forces could be sent to Hungary to try to make peace there. They say a huge statue of Stalin has been destroyed by demonstrators in Budapest and important prisoners have been freed by rioters."

"All we can do is to make sure that we do what we can in our own circle, and that means making Margaret welcome and reassured, and sending Mick and Eileen off on a well-earned holiday," said Paul.

"Our circle expands all the time. This time last year we had no idea you would have a partner and that Joan Bright would marry Robert. What a good thing it is to have a really big house that swallows up a lot of people."

"And that makes you happy?"

"Yes. We have each other and a very thriving clinic and there are a lot of people who really do like us. I am happier than I've been all my life."

"Me too, but I think this big house is going to need your full attention if you want to make your visitors comfortable. Eileen can help before she leaves for

Ireland and then, if you continue to daydream about us, I shall have to put Mrs Coster in charge!"

"At least she'll be smart in her new pinnies! . . . I must sweet-talk the butcher. We may have finished with rationing but some things are hard to get, so I must make sure of a couple of good joints of beef and lamb to feed the five thousand. I'll remind him that he has a piece of silverside in pickle for us. I hope they all like boiled beef and carrots and cold beef sandwiches."

Paul watched his wife hurry from the office, and thought how lucky he was in his married life and his work. He chewed the end of a pencil and looked sad. He hoped that Emma would not look as attractive as she did now when she talked to George, and that George really did love his new wife.

Four

Emma checked the freshly cleaned bedroom for the third time while Mrs Coster eyed her with deep suspicion. "Did I miss something, sister?"

"Everything is fine," Emma said hastily. "I was wondering if *I* had missed something, not you. Not everyone likes flowers in their bedroom, but that is only a pot plant and it does look nice there."

"They'll be in clover," Mrs Coster asserted. "You've made more fuss about this room than you did when Mrs Miller and her American husband came to stay."

"Bea is almost family – we've known each other for years – but I have to make friends with my cousin's wife."

"Don't try too hard," was Mrs Coster's advice. "Treat her like the furniture and let her help. She must be as nervous as you are as her hubby was sweet on you and probably is still a bit keen."

"Mrs Coster! That isn't true. George is happily married and has forgotten that he fancied me a little."

"If you say so." Mrs Coster sniffed eloquently.

"Any news of Sid?" Emma said to change the subject.

"He went off to his pal in Kent and said he'll stay until the harvest is over. They used to go hopping when

37

they were boys and Sid always said he might go on the land one day. Good riddance! They used to come home from the hop fields covered in dust and bits of straw and smelling like a brewery even then, as the adults had a ration of ale as part of their pay and the boys often stole some. He was getting really bad after Maisie left, but his pal knows him and won't let him drink too much. My other son is looking after the stall so he won't lose anything by not being there. Speak as you find, I say. My family stick together and help each other out and Sid has always been generous to the young 'uns so they like him."

"If Maureen could look after Rose and Clive tomorrow morning, I want to show Margaret some parts of London that she hasn't seen."

Mrs Coster shook her head. "Beg your pardon but I wouldn't. If I was you, I'd take the children to see the Guards and be a family. Kids make people laugh and be themselves, and she might enjoy it. Maureen can take over in the afternoon when they have a play and then go in the park."

"You're as wise as my Aunt Emily."

"I take that as a real compliment. I have a lot of time for your aunt, and it's time she came to stay here again."

"Mick and Eileen must be having a good time. The weather over there is warm just now. I'm anxious to know what they think of Ireland since my husband might have to give lectures over there and I shall go with him."

"Dangerous place, Ireland," Mrs Coster said with the air of a permanent resident who knew all the bad places and life-threatening incidents of the country. "You wouldn't take little Rose there, would you?"

"Of course. Eileen and Mick took Jean and had no doubts that she'd be safe and enjoy herself. When we were in America, I had a few bad moments and wondered if we were safe, but Ireland is close to home and I like Irish people."

"I can wear my best apron when they come," Mrs Coster said. "I do like the one with the frills. Rather saucy but very nice and too good to wear doing the hall."

Emma laughed. "Now who's making far too much effort for the visitors?" She looked at her watch. "Is that the time? I must get on in the kitchen if I'm not to be covered in flour when they arrive. I want to make some pasties and a lemon meringue pie."

"You've got a fridge full of nice things already, and they will be here for only four days."

"You forget that I shall be alone as far as catering is concerned. I think I depend on Eileen more than I realised."

"That's her job, and you have enough to do with the clinic and entertaining Dr Paul's doctor friends, but I must say Eileen has come on well from the poor little thing she was when Mick brought her here. She couldn't say boo to a goose and had no idea about cooking."

Emma made pastry and left it ready to use while she cut up steak, potato, onion and a little turnip for the pasties, and soon the smell of baking leaked out of the kitchen.

"Close the door or you'll have all my patients wanting to stay for lunch," Paul said as he sat on the edge of the kitchen table and munched a piece of pie that had fallen off as it was lifted from the baking sheet.

"Busy?" she asked with a disbelieving smile. "No! That pasty isn't a misshape and you'll have to wait an hour for lunch, unless George and Margaret arrive early and hungry."

"You've got flour on your eyebrow," he said tenderly and kissed her. "I've never seen you make pastry without getting paler and paler with white streaks in your hair."

She dashed to the mirror over the kitchen sink and turned to deny it, but Paul had escaped back to his consulting room where Robert was waiting to talk to him.

The last of the baking was finished and Emma smoothed her hair and hoped she didn't look too hot. She moved restlessly about the house, twitching a curtain into position, rearranging flowers and making sure the table was set for lunch.

Why am I on edge? she wondered. We have a lot of visitors and these are family so it should be easy; but she remembered the expression in George's eyes when they had last met. He had regarded her sadly, with a lingering memory of his earlier love for her.

That was before he married Margaret, she told herself crossly. He told me that he loved her, and they've had time to settle into married life and forget any hitches in their separate pasts.

Rose wandered into the kitchen, sleepy from her nap. "Has Mark come yet?" she asked.

Emma hugged her, revelling in her softness and the smell of flower-scented talcum powder. "Not Mark, darling. It's Clive who's coming to stay, and they should be here very soon, so why not go down to Mrs Coster and wait for them?"

Rose held up a sandal. Emma adjusted the buckle on the one that Rose had managed for herself and made sure that both were secure. "I'll be careful on the stairs," Rose said, anticipating her mother's concern, and Emma shrugged: one more sign that Rose was growing up into independence. And when, five minutes later, Clive burst into the hall and Rose gave squeals of delight, she knew that Rose was badly in need of a brother or sister.

"Margaret! This is a real pleasure," Emma said warmly and hugged the rather pale woman who came into the hall with George behind her. "It's good to see you, George." She raised her face to brush his cheek in a formal kiss then turned back to his wife. "Come in and leave your cases for us to take to your bedroom."

"I'll help you up with it," Mrs Coster said, and Emma saw that the frilly apron was being flaunted in all its full glory.

"Let her do it," Emma whispered, "and please say that her apron is pretty!"

Margaret relaxed. "How kind of you, Mrs Coster, but isn't that lovely apron too smart for heavy work?"

"All the way from America," Mrs Coster said proudly, and stomped up the stairs with two cases, obviously delighted that Margaret knew her name and had noticed how smart she looked.

"You have a slave for life," Emma remarked with a smile. "All our guests have to be approved by Mrs Coster, and those who don't pass get very funny looks at times."

41

"I didn't realise *she* was in charge!"

Paul laughed. "That's the least of it. If she takes a dislike to certain patients she tells me what she thinks should be their diagnosis – and sometimes she's right!"

"Clive seems to have disappeared with Rose, so we have time for a drink before lunch, if Paul has finished?"

"All done, and Robert can join us for five minutes before he goes to lunch at Guy's."

"Can I help?" asked George.

"If you would. It's all there, I think. Lots of gin and mixers but a bit short on whiskey."

"I'll show you your rooms, Margaret," Emma said. "When we bought this house it seemed far too big for just two people and a consulting room, but now we fill it all and it's good to have visitors who know that they can do as they want without falling over us."

"It's lovely and has a very home-like atmosphere," Margaret said rather sadly. "I do love my work, but sometimes I wish that George and I had started with a home of our own."

"Is the house in Hampshire nearly ready? Aunt Janey said the two apartments were nearly finished and then you'll have your own place to furnish and arrange to your liking." Emma glanced at her guest. "I know Janey and Alex are looking forward to having you close to them when you're on leave, and I shall be relieved that Janey has a real friend to keep an eye on her as her arthritis is bad now."

"She's very independent and I wonder if she really does want me there."

"She needs you, Margaret," Emma said gently. "She

has reservations about the arrangement too, but it's hard for anyone as active as Janey to admit she needs help. She has enough domestic help to limit what anyone else has to do for her and Alex is wonderful, helping out with anything heavy. He has learned to cook when Janey's hands are swollen. Don't feel that she doesn't want you there. She hates the thought that you might feel obligated to them in any way and so holds back a little."

"They have done so much for us, giving us half their house and making it so comfortable."

"You have a flat in their house for when you need it but you forget that Janey will be for ever in *your* debt for lending her Clive to look after," Emma said firmly. "She thinks that it is wonderful as she found that with Alex as her husband she could never have more children. George is her only child and she'd wanted a big family. Clive makes up for a lot, especially as he reminds her of her first husband."

"I think she wants us there because of George, not me."

Emma saw the tense line of Margaret's mouth and sighed inwardly, but managed to smile. "My aunts are similar in many ways. They were brought up in a large family that generated its own happiness, but my grandfather was a hard man and discouraged any outward show of real affection. It wasn't difficult for some of the family to be like him. I know, as my own mother was a selfish and unloving woman, but Emily and Janey are different. They have a lot of love that they seldom show, except towards the children. Even now I'm allowed to hug Aunt Emily about once a year," she added lightly. "But she lets

43

Rose sit on her lap and hug her and I know that she really does love me very much."

Margaret looked surprised. "I can hardly believe that. She talks of you with great pride and affection each time we're there, and George's mother does too."

"That I can believe, but although they're devoted sisters they never kiss or hug each other and are not well disposed to strangers who try to be over-affectionate."

Paul called that their drinks were getting warm, and Margaret followed Emma, looking pensive.

Joan Bright handed out the drinks and Margaret was introduced to her and Robert. Clive and Rose were giggling over tumblers half full of orange squash which they were drinking noisily through straws; Paul watched them with a wry smile.

"They look good together," Margaret said with sudden warmth.

"Children do make a difference," Paul said, and glanced at his wife. Emma looked away: she knew he wanted another child, but there was no sign of one on the way even though she'd given up birth control since returning from America.

George stirred the ice bucket and took another ice cube for his drink. He smiled at his wife. "Margaret is wonderful with Clive and he loves her, so we have a family ready made."

Robert moved closer to Margaret and offered to freshen her drink but she shook her head. "That's something we both face in the future," he said quietly. "Joan and I have just become engaged, and I am anxious to know how it feels for a woman with a good career to give it up when she has a child. You may have to do that, I suppose, as Joan certainly will, unless you don't want your own children?"

"I want my own baby," she said with sudden passion. "I want a baby made by George and me." She blushed. "I am very fond of Clive, but I want our own baby and until we have that I shall not be safe."

"Not safe?" he asked gently, and she found that somehow they were sitting on a settee slightly away from the rest.

Margaret held her empty glass so tightly that Robert thought it must snap, so he took it from her hand. "I am in love with my husband and I want a family of our own but I can't be certain of anything." She looked at him questioningly. "Why did I tell you that?"

"Because we have much in common over this matter, and because people do talk to me."

"Why you, when I can't talk about this to George?"

"He's too close; I am not involved, but I have ears and sympathy."

She smiled weakly. "You're a doctor, so you know about people and their thoughts. Don't you find that a terrible burden?"

"Not often, and sometimes a doctor gains help for himself from talking to patients, in unexpected ways."

"I don't see that we have similar problems."

"Not the same problems, but there are some that concern the physical and mental welfare of two women faced with the loss of their careers when they bow to the needs of marriage and parenthood." He eyed her with interest. "Joan is luckier than you in that respect. She can carry on working in some capacity even after we have children. My clinic will need her and she will always meet people in her own profession through our mutual contacts, but you will leave the Navy and be . . . no, not 'just a housewife', but a much loved wife and mother, a homemaker."

"A housewife would be more correct!" She turned her face towards Robert, her eyes wet and her mouth contorted with anguish.

"You have a loving husband and you are in love with him, Margaret. The rest will follow."

"You don't understand! He says he loves me but he isn't mine completely."

"I believe he was a widower when he married you, and Clive is the child of that marriage?" Robert sounded as if he had heard only sketchy details of her past.

"I love Clive; there will never be the wicked stepmother syndrome between us."

"I suppose it's natural to wonder what Sadie was like," he suggested.

"Sadie?" Margaret looked blank. "Sadie wasn't important, except for the fact that she gave George a son. Janey doesn't talk about her with any affection: she thought she was shallow and selfish behind that glamorous façade and she was sure the marriage wouldn't last."

Robert smiled his understanding. "So you came along and made George really happy, being not only the wife he wanted but a WREN officer, a companion from the same naval background."

"You can forget Sadie. I think George did that very quickly. She was pretty enough to make any man want her, but so are hundreds of sexy girls he meets in the services."

"What then?" Robert asked gently. "What more have you to face?"

"Nothing." She stood up and walked over to George.

He put an arm round her shoulders and smiled down at her. "How's my girl?" he said.

"Fine," she replied. "Did I hear someone call us for lunch?"

"I have to go to the hospital, or they'll have eaten all the food," Robert said. "It's an informal buffet and shop-talk, but the average medico is a starving gannet and it's survival of the fittest there." He grinned. "I'll be in tomorrow morning." He glanced at Margaret. "We must talk again," he said. "I enjoyed meeting you, and I think George is a very lucky man."

"I second that," George said, and when he smiled at his wife it was plain to see his sincerity, but Margaret blushed in sudden confusion, as if he'd made a remark that she welcomed but couldn't quite believe.

Lunch was lightened by the presence of the two children who were excited at the prospect of seeing the Changing of the Guard at Buckingham Palace and the waxworks at Madame Tussaud's.

"Not all on one day," Emma warned them. "We'll be worn out, and Margaret and I want to see the shops."

"Oh, *no*," they groaned. Clive was sitting next to Margaret and looked at her with pleading eyes. "We *are* going to see the Maritime Museum, aren't we?"

She smiled. "I wouldn't miss it for the world."

"Thanks, Maggie Mum," he said and hugged her, to the detriment of the forkful of salad she held in her hand.

"Maggie Mum?" George looked amused and puzzled. "When did you decide on that name?"

"She told me she wasn't my real mother so I can't call her Mummy or Mother, and she's not just a relative like Auntie Emma. We had to think of something nice as she's my friend."

"I see." George lifted an eyebrow and laughed. "I wondered how long it would be before you both came to some kind of decision and that does do as well as any, if you like the name Maggie. Why Maggie?"

"She said she was called Maggie at school and I like it," Clive said with satisfaction. "I like having a Maggie Mum who is a kind of sailor and likes boats."

Emma smiled. So I'm just a relative, she thought. It put distance between her and her cousin George in a natural way. "When you see the scarlet uniforms and huge bearskin hats tomorrow you may want to be a soldier instead of a sailor," she said.

Clive looked at her as if trying to convince a baby of limited intelligence that he knew best. "You don't understand. We're sailors in our family, aren't we, Daddy?"

"Yes, sailors are different," George agreed.

Five

E mma parked the car in St James's and Margaret handed the bulging brown paper bags to the children. "We can't see the Guards for another half an hour, so we'll feed the ducks in the park first."

Rose skipped down the broad steps into the park and ran over to the lake, followed by Clive who, being older, tried to appear unmoved by the excitement of the morning. The leaves were dark and the grass had yellow patches where many feet had trodden. The area round the bandstand was almost bare after the dry spell, and Emma felt as if autumn was not far away, but knew that it was in her mind rather than a reality as there were likely to be several weeks of hot weather to come before the chill started.

Ducks of every description fought and chivvied each other as they saw the crusts being thrown from the bridge. The water was turbulent with bright feathers and quacking beaks.

"I want that one with the green feathers to have my bread," Rose stated, and was delighted when he roughly thrust away a couple of dowdier birds. She looked at Emma with sparkling eyes. "Why don't we come here sometimes, Mummy?"

"I thought this park was very popular, especially with children," Margaret said.

"We use the park nearer home, and they like to look at Peter Pan," Emma said. "I came here a lot when I was training. It was a place where friends arranged to meet, just as the National Gallery was a good place if it was raining."

"Had you forgotten how much you enjoyed it?" Margaret eyed her with curiosity. "Or is it a place that you want to forget, because it holds memories . . . as it does for me?"

Emma glanced at her sharply. "Times change, people come and go and some meetings all over the West End were good and some bad. You're right. There are memories here that are firmly in the past, mostly to do with my fiancé, who died in Belsen, trying to help in terrible conditions when the camp was liberated. I don't often actively remember him and other friends I made during the war but sometimes, in old haunts, I feel sad, as if remnants of happy and miserable times are there beyond a veil."

"I know exactly what you mean. I came here on leave with my fiancé and we had so little time to discover each other." She laughed. "I swear the ducks are the same ones we fed all that time ago, but I haven't been here since then."

"How strange," Emma said slowly. "You and I have both been engaged to men who died, but now have husbands who are right for us." She smiled. "We're the lucky ones, and when I look at Rose and think that she might never have been born I am deeply grateful to whoever arranges such things."

"Did you miss him very much?"

"Paul was there in the background, ready to help and hoping I would fall in love with him, which I did, and realised that he was a better, kinder man and would make a better father than Guy would have done."

Margaret looked across the lake as if she wanted to keep her mind detached from the woman at her side. "Were there other men?"

Emma made herself answer calmly. "A childhood sweetheart who was just a warm friend and not really for me; one or two patients who swore undying love; and I was asked to marry a wealthy man who had a manor house, horses and all the trimmings of rich country and county life. But I think that one's own heart dictates what is suitable and I turned him down, much to his mother's chagrin, as she thought he should have turned *me* down."

"That must have been fun." Margaret smiled more normally. "I've met women like that, high-ranking service wives who can be very arrogant."

Will she mention George? Emma wondered. "And you? As an attractive woman you must have had other boyfriends?"

"A few, before I was engaged, but I confess that when I met George, which was before my fiancé died, I fell in love with him and in my heart I knew I couldn't marry the man who thought I was in love with, even if I never saw George again." She took a deep breath. "George ruined any other man for me, and I couldn't believe it when he seemed to like me a lot and was sympathetic when my fiancé died, but I never thought fate would let me marry him."

"George was your fate, as Paul is mine," Emma said. "We have the future settled as far as love and contentment go."

Margaret screwed up the paper bags that were now empty and gave them to Clive to put in the rubbish bin. "If only it was that simple," she murmured. "Come along, children. Time to watch the smart soldiers. We'll walk along the Mall and soon we'll hear the band."

Emma paused to button the jacket that Rose had undone earlier.

What had Margaret meant? Life was now much simpler for her. She was married to a man she adored and who obviously loved her, she had health and a career that she could follow or give up at any time she wanted to leave it, and she had a future with no obvious clouds to make her depressed, and yet her insecurity was palpable.

"Look, Mummy!" Rose put her face to the palace railings while Clive tried to appear nonchalant, as if he saw the tall, bearskin-hatted men every day. "It's just like Christopher Robin in the song," Rose said, enchanted with the scene. "I wonder which Guard is the one Alice is going to marry?"

"He might be off duty," Emma reasoned.

"Or pensioned off, if he's that old," Margaret whispered and the two women giggled, finding a rapport that had not been there when they fed the ducks.

The spark of humour and the spontaneous giggle transformed Margaret's face, and Emma saw the pretty girl whom George now loved. "We can have something to eat in a Lyon's Corner House, unless you know a better place," Emma suggested. "It's ages since I came here, but it used to be a convenient place where girls could eat unmolested by men trying to pick up young nurses and servicewomen. The crimson plush and neat tables in the Vienna Café, with the waitresses who were nicknamed 'nippies', dressed in black and white, were a sanctuary for a girl alone or with another off-duty nurse."

"It was cheap, too," Margaret added. "And filling! Did you have Danish pastries as big as cartwheels with lots of lovely marzipan goo leaking from the coils?"

"I want a cartwheel," Clive said. He slipped a hand into hers and looked up at Margaret with an ingratiating smile. "Can I, Maggie Mum?"

"Oh dear, George says I exaggerate. Maybe they're only as big as ordinary buns, but we'll see what they have."

"We'll have to walk along to the one in the Strand; I heard the old Coventry Street restaurant might not be there any more. They've made the new one as much like the old as far as possible, with the old-style uniforms and green and cream tablecloths and trimmings."

"If they are going back to old times, they may have the kind of pre-war sweets they sold then. If they have any, we'll take a box of Nippy Chocolates back to Daddy," Margaret promised.

"I'll take some for *my* daddy," Rose said. "Then he'll give me some."

Margaret laughed and Emma inwardly blessed Mrs

Coster for suggesting that this kind of outing was better than having Margaret to herself in an adult situation, just looking round shops and perhaps a museum.

"Do we have to go back for lunch?" Margaret asked.

"No, I told Paul not to wait for us. The three men are capable of finding food and there's plenty of cold meat and salad and fresh bread, so let's have something here."

"Clive seldom has a meal in a café, as Janey insists that she can provide better and more suitable food at home, and most of his outings are close to home, with no real excuse for cafés, so this will be a treat."

"I do like you, Maggie Mum," Clive said, and forgot that he was much too old to hold an adult's hand. As they crossed Trafalgar Square he held on to Margaret with an unusual show of affection.

Rose stared up at the Landseer lions and stayed close to Emma. Pigeons gathered as each new party of people crossed the square, and Clive wished he'd saved some bread for them, but Rose thought they were too big and bossy and hurried to get past the fat, strutting birds.

Emma glanced up at the façade of the National Gallery where she had met so many people during the war.

"There must be thousands of ghosts milling around those steps," Margaret said. "Some of people in love, some tragic, and all a part of London in wartime."

"I remember," Emma agreed and thought of Philip, the RAF officer who'd come down in the sea off the coast of India and nearly died. It had wrung her heart when he appeared on those steps, gaunt, uniform hung on him, but recovering as far as his physical condition was concerned. He'd still wanted to marry her, even though she'd refused him long before his accident, but she knew she couldn't do so, however much she pitied him. "Come on, before we get maudlin!"

The open-slatted stairs curved up to a second floor and the whole restaurant was bathed in light. Rose unfolded the pale green table napkin and then tried to make another shape of it but finally placed it across her lap as she saw Emma do and picked up the menu. "What does this say, Mummy?"

"It tells us what there is to eat," Clive said in a superior voice. "I can read it."

Margaret read from another menu. "Not a lot of choice, but the children will like it," she said. "What's it to be? Sardines on toast, beans on toast, spaghetti on toast, egg and chips or fish and chips? I don't think we'll risk lamb chop and peas or pork pie and chips. I like to know what goes into pies and how long the lamb has been running on the hills!"

"Not fish either," Emma said. "We can get some tomorrow from our local fish and chip shop and it's very good."

"I can't see cartwheels." Clive was disappointed.

"Try Danish pastries," Emma suggested. "We can have them for pudding."

The Danish pastries were as Emma remembered them: fresh and delicious with thin white icing and lots of sultanas. They bought some to take home, even though Emma knew that by evening they wouldn't be as fresh.

"I must be getting old. That bun gave me heartburn," Margaret said.

"They *are* very filling," Emma admitted, but the children had eaten one each and couldn't wait to take the others home to eat later.

They bought small boxes of chocolates and candies, each with the picture of a "nippy" waitress on the cover, and went back to the car as Rose showed signs of needing a nap. Emma drove back to Kensington and Margaret yawned as if she too was tired. George came to meet them and kissed his wife. "I missed you," he said.

"We saw the Guards," Clive told him, "and I had beans for lunch."

"We fed the ducks and I had sardines and a big, big bun," Rose added, not to be outdone.

George laughed. "You make me envious."

"Let's give Daddy his sweets," Emma said and followed Rose up to the office. Robert left Paul and Rose to open the chocolates and eyed Emma with interest. "How did it go?" he asked.

Emma frowned. "We had a very good morning and the children were very excited. They're tourists in the making, and even Clive was impressed by the marching and the uniforms."

"And Margaret?"

Emma met Robert's steady gaze and shrugged. "Fine, I think, but she's not entirely happy. She said a curious thing when I said that George was her fate and Paul was mine and we were lucky. She muttered something but I did catch one sentence. She said, 'If only it was that simple,' and sounded bitter."

56

"George went down to meet you and seemed eager to see Margaret again."

"He loves her, Robert. It's quite obvious, but I don't think she believes him."

"He didn't pay a lot of attention to you while Margaret was there yesterday and I had a long chat with her. I agree that she's insecure, and maybe I should talk with her again." He grinned. "If you're anything like most nurses I've met, you're now dying for a cup of tea. Joan would rather have tea than the best champagne, which is good as I don't think we can afford champagne on a regular basis," he said lightly. "She accepts that I make a good cuppa so I'll do just that and you can make sure that Margaret stays to join us. See you in five minutes in the sitting room."

"No thanks, Clive. I won't have another sweet. That bun was very big and I doubt if I'll want anything more to eat today." Margaret accepted the cup offered and Robert sat companionably by her side, sipping his tea. "Tell me about this morning," he suggested. "How do the children fit in together? I once had a cousin who everyone told me that I would like to have as a friend and we hated each other on sight," he said cheerfully.

"Nothing like that with Clive and Rose," Margaret said warmly. "They have a nice easy relationship and find the same things funny. Emma is very good with both of them and is careful not to favour Rose too much when Clive is with her."

"That's important. Clive could have had a very rough time after his mother died and his father had to go back on duty. I know he doesn't remember his mother but she must have left a gap that a father alone couldn't fill. Relatives are so important, and now Clive is a very normal little boy with no petty jealousies or chips on his shoulder thanks to his great-aunts and now you."

"And Emma?"

"I doubt if she had much contact with Clive, as she saw very little of George except when she visited her aunt on the Isle of Wight." He refilled Margaret's cup and sat down again. "Emma has had her own problems that were no concern of George's and she didn't have the time or inclination to take on a cousin's child."

"What problems?" Margaret showed her disbelief. "She always seems so happy and settled, as if nothing could stir her calm. I think she could have anything or anyone she wanted."

"She has a vast experience of people through her work and the war and she has suffered from Guy's death and her own arid family life with parents who were cold. She recognises true values and would never take what wasn't hers to take or encourage anyone to come closer than was advisable or necessary. She's seen enough suffering to make her cautious about people and has no intention of adding to any other person's heartache." He watched her face. "Did you know that Rose was a miracle to her, as she thought she could never have children?"

"George has never mentioned it."

"Why should he? If he did know, then it was still none of his business, except for his interest in Emma as a cousin. He had his own life to find after Sadie. He found you, and thank God you love each other – it's so clear that you do."

"I do love him."

"And he loves you," Robert said simply. "He loves his wife and has no place in his life for any other woman. You also love Clive, and that binds you even closer to George."

She gave a shuddering sigh. "You must think I'm a suspicious fool, or depressed and incapable of believing in the good things," she said. "I know he loves me and yet I don't know how deep it is with him."

"I think you have been hurt in the past and so has George." Robert laughed. "You may have had good friends who comforted you, but George had only his relatives, and older women can be a little maudlin and not what a suffering, active man requires."

Her eyes held an accusation. "He had Emma."

"Emma? No. Emma has had no part in his life except as a warm friend. She was an only child, like George, and missed having siblings. George is a good friend, although they have met so seldom. And there is a family link that helps take away any atmosphere between a man and a woman, making a relationship safe: there could never be a sexual link."

"You think that blood relations are different?"

"Truly, if they have integrity. The ancient laws have it right, and most people know instinctively that it is so." He stood and looked down at her with a stern expression. "Love and care for him, and you will find out how much he loves you, but never insult him by hinting he has any unworthy thoughts about another woman."

Margaret began to sob quietly. "I think I hate you," she said, then dried her eyes. "A part of me wanted to blame Emma for any imagined neglect that George might show me, but I can't blame her, and I don't want to. I like her."

"Are you all right?" Robert asked her.

"I'm feeling rather emotional today, that's all."

"Because you went out with Emma?"

"No. Strangely enough I did enjoy that, and I was relaxed with her and the children, but now I'm tired; I'll go to bed early."

"Margaret doesn't want any dinner," George said later. "She's in bed reading, and I'll take some hot milk in later. What did you have for lunch that was such a huge meal? Usually my wife can eat more than I can!"

"She said the Danish pastry was too big and gave her heartburn," Emma said, and regarded the now limp and unappetising buns with distaste. "Do you think anyone will eat them, or shall I throw them away?"

"I'm starving! They look OK to me," George said and selected the one with the most marzipan. He grinned. "I know! Granny would have said I'm greedy and a bun now will spoil my dinner, but I didn't have much lunch as I had to make a few emergency phone calls and could only grab a sandwich."

"Duty?" Emma asked.

"I have to see a couple of brass hats tomorrow morning at the Admiralty and needed to get some information. It may not be a crisis but I could have to go away." He looked serious. "Is it all right if Margaret stays on for a while until her leave is up? She's due back in four days and we would have travelled together but I may not be going back to Bath."

"She can stay as long as necessary," Emma said, smiling. "I hope Clive can stay on too. Rose adores him and it's helped to take her mind off Bea's family in America."

"You are a gem . . . but I always knew that." His smile was wicked and Emma shook her head slightly. George must never look at her like that again, even in fun.

"Eat up your bun and don't blame me if you have hiccups all evening," she said severely.

"Yes, Aunt Emily," he said. "You frighten me when you sound like her!"

"Good."

"Buns?" Robert pulled a piece of soggy pastry away from the rest of the bun and ate it with every sign of enjoyment.

"Not you too? I think they look revolting after being sat on by Rose in the car."

"Just what I need. I'm meeting Joan for a late supper when she comes off duty and, as one of my patients said when he had everything by mouth withheld before a test, 'Come on, Doc, let me have a bit of something. My stomach thinks me throat's been cut.' I shall feel the same by nine o'clock."

Paul left the office and joined them. "Where's Margaret?"

"She's gone to bed. Nothing terrible, just tired,"

George said with more vehemence than seemed necessary. "No headache and no temperature, just catching up after a busy day."

"I'll go in and ask her if she wants anything before we have dinner," Emma said casually. "George, make yourself useful and mash the potatoes in that saucepan, and then we'll be ready."

Paul eyed her with speculation and followed her from the kitchen. "Anything wrong?"

"I'm sure there is nothing but George hates illness and when Sadie died you remember how she was . . . Tired and listless before the temperature soared and she died of meningitis. George must dread anything that could harm his second wife, a woman who is usually fairly tough."

"So you made him mash potatoes while you cast an expert eye over her?"

She tapped on the bedroom door and opened it. "Have you changed your mind and could eat some beef?" Emma asked. "George and Robert have both eaten some squashed buns so there will be plenty of beef left over if they have indigestion."

"I feel a fraud. I had a nap and now I do feel hungry. I'll be dressed in five minutes."

Emma breathed an inaudible sigh of relief and the ghost of Sadie fled. "No headache?"

"Not now," Margaret said and reached for her clothes. "Just a kind of lethargy. I think I must be overtired." She rubbed her cheeks to take away the pallor and applied a bright lipstick before emerging for dinner.

Six

"Up so early?" Paul yawned. "And tea? It isn't my birthday or a national holiday is it?"

"I slept well and we were all in bed earlier than usual as Margaret was tired and George has to go to the Admiralty, so I thought an early breakfast would be welcome, unless you want stale Danish pastries?"

"I think I've eaten my ration of them for at least five years," Paul said with feeling. "If you have any more relics of nostalgic wartime food, do you mind trying them on Mrs Coster or someone else with a cast-iron stomach first?"

"You feel all right?"

Paul swung his legs out of the bed and stretched. "Only teasing. I never felt better. Come here."

"Paul!" Emma protested when at last he released her. "I didn't know Danish pastries had *that* effect."

"Buy some more and we'll set up a serious experiment."

Emma kissed him and rumpled his hair. "Breakfast in half an hour when I'm more suitably dressed." She belted her dressing-gown firmly and made for the shower.

Emma heard muted sounds from the bathroom on

63

the other side of the partition wall that separated the original bathroom into two shower rooms, one for her use and one for the guest room. She turned on the taps and hurried over her shower, thinking that George might want breakfast really early.

She dressed and was busy in the kitchen when George appeared. She laughed at his sleepy expression. "Bacon and eggs and toast, or are you another who ate too many buns yesterday?"

He looked blank for a moment and then smiled as if relieved. "That's what it was. Bacon and eggs sounds fine, as I have no idea if the top brass will give me lunch, but Margaret wants to stay in bed for a while and doesn't want breakfast. Now I know why."

"Those buns have a lot to answer for," Emma said. "Margaret said she had heartburn after she'd eaten one but I enjoyed mine. Obviously Clive and Rose haven't been affected. It's good that they will eat anything and aren't faddy over food."

Paul joined them, looking pensive.

"Anything wrong?" asked Emma.

"No, I was just thinking," he replied blandly. She gave him a sharp look, but he didn't share his thoughts with them. He asked what time George was due for his appointment and offered to drive him as he had no patient booked until ten o'clock. "We'll leave soon, as I think you need to be there."

George nodded and went to fetch his briefcase. He came back putting on the cap that completed his smart naval uniform. "Margaret's asleep, so tell her I said goodbye."

Emma watched them leave and slowly climbed the stairs out of the kitchen, then hurried to the nursery where Clive had a bed and Rose still had her divan with the cot sides. She helped Rose to dress and sent Clive to wash but warned him that he mustn't disturb Margaret as she was still asleep.

Rose and Clive were settled with cereal and toast and Emma was drinking a second cup of tea when she heard Margaret moving about outside the kitchen. She opened the door and gasped. Margaret was in her nightie, looking pale and trembling. "Back to bed; I'll get a hot-water bottle," Emma said briskly. "You look frozen."

"I'll be fine," Margaret said. "I'm better now, but I think I will have another nap."

Once in bed her colour returned to normal. When Emma made her suck a thermometer all was as it should be.

"I must have had a tummy upset," Margaret said. "I woke up feeling terrible and while George was having breakfast I was sick."

"Do you still feel like that?" Emma asked casually.

"No, and can I be very awkward and have some toast or something? I'm warm now and don't want to stay here."

"I'll put the kettle on again and make toast, unless you'd like an egg and bacon?"

"Just toast and marmalade and tea would be wonderful. Whatever it was that made me sick must have gone; I feel hungry now."

When Paul ran up the stairs fifteen minutes later Margaret was still eating and talking to Emma. "Good.

You haven't cleared away. I think I'll have some more toast," he said and laughed when Emma tried to slice another reasonable piece of bread from the end of a loaf that had been badly plundered. "I'll have the crust," he offered and piled it high with marmalade. "George is safely settled at the Admiralty and, from the look of several gleaming motors setting down a lot of caps with scrambled eggs and gold bands on uniforms, there's a lot of activity there today."

"It's almost certain that we'll move big ships into the Suez area," Margaret said calmly. "I packed a bag for George last week and brought it here as it could happen without more warning. We wondered if it would be today."

"George is very fortunate to have you to understand what naval personnel have to do," Paul said. "If you need someone to take you to him to say goodbye, Robert is free this morning and has no cases so he's at your disposal as soon as he arrives here."

"I'd like that," Margaret said, with a slight smile. "Robert is a very nice person. I'm sure his patients must respond to him very quickly and feel they can trust him."

The telephone seemed extra loud and insistent; Paul went to answer it. He closed the door to the office and listened. At last he said, "I advise you to stay there, George. You haven't a lot of time and Margaret will want to see you alone, not with a crowd of your relatives." He listened again. "I'm sure Robert will find the club, and you and Margaret can have a few hours together in private. She has your case and we all wish you the best of luck. We'll look after her for as long as she wants to stay with us." He put down the receiver and returned to the kitchen. "Action stations," he said cheerfully. "I heard Robert downstairs so I'll brief him if you want to get ready for him to take you."

"George isn't coming back here?"

Paul grinned. "I know I'd feel the same. He wants his wife alone for the few hours before he has to report on duty and he suggested his club in St James's. A private room with lunch there was what he had in mind, so don't hang about!"

"You almost *pushed* her out," Emma complained. "And don't we have a chance to say goodbye to George?"

"I think Aunt Emily would approve," Paul said complacently.

"Do you really believe I'd hug him with tears in my eyes and say how much I'll miss him?" she retorted.

"No, but he might have done something to make Margaret think things!"

"That's ridiculous."

"There's something more. You noticed that he was on edge when he thought that his wife was not well and had a headache and lethargy last night?"

"I confess I was anxious too. It was so like Sadie and the onset of her fatal attack, but I took her temperature and pulse and after that brief nap this morning she was fine." Emma looked anxious. "George must go away as happy about her as possible."

"He will be after this last private meeting. She looks blooming, and so in love."

"And pleased that she'll have him all to herself? Who suggested the club for their farewells?"

"I did mention that they'd have more privacy there, and he took the hint and told me to say goodbye to you."

"Thanks. I enjoy offhand, long-distance goodbyes," she said drily.

Paul looked into her eyes. "They'll be fine, but I wanted him out of the way this morning before he got worried again."

"You heard her being sick?"

He nodded.

"Sick first thing in the morning, doctor?"

"You think so, too."

"Yes, but Margaret has no idea and we must keep quiet until she's convinced she's pregnant. If George is away for a month or so, he can come back to a loving wife who has forgotten the morning sickness and is healthy and active."

"A little bit sad?" Paul kissed her tenderly. "We have Rose, and she's more than we thought possible so don't worry. If we are to have another child, it will happen, but if it makes you more settled, why not see Stella again and have an examination?"

"I thought about it, but wanted to leave it until we'd been back in England for a while. I tried to convince myself that my body wasn't ready for change after all the travelling." She smiled. "I know that's not true. I can't put it off and I think a visit to Beattie's might be in order now."

"Don't ring her yet. Maybe, if we're right, Margaret

might want a consultation to confirm her condition, unless she would rather have a naval doctor to see her."

"We're jumping to conclusions," Emma said. "It might have been a tummy upset."

"Mind where you're walking," Mrs Coster said in the hall. "Oh, it's you, Dr Forsyth. That's all right then."

She wrung out the floor cloth and stood up. "Gone to war, has he? My Maureen said that a sailor she knows had to report back to his ship and I told her not to get too sorry for him. You know what sailors are," she added darkly.

Robert grinned. "I'm sure that Maureen wouldn't fall for that sort of chat-up line, and it may be a false alarm and George will be back again later."

"His missus won't like it if he goes away just now."

"Why now in particular? She's in the Navy too, and knows that he might be sent away at any time."

Emma paused on the stairs and laughed. "Mrs Coster, you're as bad as my Aunt Emily, but this time you could be wrong."

Mrs Coster wiped her nose with the back of her hand and picked up her bucket. "You mark my words, Sister."

"What's all this? Am I missing something?" Robert asked plaintively.

The two women looked at him with superior pity. "And he's a doctor," Emma said.

Robert still looked blank, and Mrs Coster began to sing in a reedy, out-of-tune voice, "Rock-a-bye baby in the tree tops."

"How do you know?" he asked.

"Sick this morning, and, as my Aunt Emily would say, it shows in her face."

"What I like is a purely scientific diagnosis," Robert said.

"Come and have some coffee and leave the two witches to their spells," Paul called. "All safely delivered?" he asked.

"I can't wait to be married," Robert said. "It must let you lose all your inhibitions and life must be wonderful."

"It is," Paul said. "Margaret has a little way to go before she can really relax and believe that George loves her alone, but it's coming, and if they are expecting a baby as we suspect, that will make them really close."

"They were very happy when I left them. George said he'd put Margaret into a service car to bring her back here when he leaves, and that might be early this evening."

"Meanwhile I have work to do," Emma said.

"Can you spare half an hour first?" Paul glanced at the papers on the office desk.

"You need a chaperone?"

"Normally Mick would be here, but I need someone, and you especially, to gather your own opinions of the patient."

"Is he new?"

"I saw him before we went away and he wanted to see me again."

"Not Robert?"

"He wouldn't come to the clinic while I was away but now says he needs me urgently."

Emma's lips twitched. "I'll be there right beside you, doctor," she said. "Now what do I need to put in the consulting room so that I have no need to leave you alone with him? A carafe of water, a few fruit pastilles, a small cushion, a spare larger cushion and a warm rug in case he has hypnosis. I can't think of anything else, can you?"

"Let's hope that's enough," Paul said drily.

"You shouldn't be so devastatingly handsome," Emma teased him.

"I've asked Mrs Coster to bring him up here as soon as he arrives. The last time he came he wandered about the place into rooms where he knew he had no right to be and was late for his appointment. I think I hear Mrs Coster now."

"It's all part of the service," they heard and Paul grinned.

"She's using her West End voice, and I bet she's wearing the frilly apron."

"Ah, Mr Symonds. What can I do for you? It's so long since you came here that I'd come to the conclusion you needed no further treatment. I think I would like to make a few more notes." Paul had his hands full of papers and seemed not to notice the eager hand held out in an effort to grasp his. "Would you mind, sister?"

Emma nodded and helped Mr Symonds off with his jacket, untied his shoelaces and settled him on the couch.

"I haven't been well," the patient began.

"You could have seen Dr Forsyth while I was away."

"Not the same. I wanted the personal touch. I'm a very sensitive man, doctor, and I took to you as soon as I saw you." He smiled. "I like to think you felt the same, and so I waited."

"If you felt ill it was unwise to postpone an appointment," Paul said calmly. He took a pad and pen and Emma sat on the chair beside the couch while Paul sat further away. "I have your previous medical history from the hospital, but it helps to fill in a little of your background. What hobbies have you?"

"I don't bother with hobbies."

"How do you fill your spare time?"

"I go to a club after work and chat to friends, and some of them come round to my place for drinks."

"Do you have many friends?"

"They come and go, and some just don't understand me, doctor. I need people who really care about me but it's hard at times."

"Have you a girlfriend? Girls are often better at caring for people. Sometimes that's true of sisters too. Did you have sisters?"

"I have two sisters who are horrible to me. They laugh at me and call me names and they don't let their children play with me. I like children," he added as if that was a real plus in his favour. "I won't have my sisters in my flat, and when I had to go to court they didn't want to know."

He stopped, as if he'd said too much. Paul made a note and referred to a case history on the desk, then looked at the man on the couch with no change of expression. "I want to ask you about that. You were referred to this clinic by the court and I made an assessment at the time, but you didn't accept treatment and later, when I was away, you refused analysis."

"Could you go and get me a glass of water, nurse?"

Emma walked over to the table and poured a glass of water from the carafe. She handed it to the man, who looked very cross. "I want to talk to the doctor alone, nurse," he said.

"You may speak freely while the sister is here, Mr Symonds. What is your story about the court appearance? I have notes from the police psychiatrist but I want to hear what you have to say."

"That man wrote a lot of lies! I was up for shoplifting and he wrote that rubbish instead."

"Shoplifting at night in a public lavatory?" Paul raised his eyebrows.

"They had no right to show you that rubbish. It was all lies. I nicked some things from the shop and got taken short and had to go to the lavatory, that's all. That's why I was there, and a nosy copper nicked me."

"They arrested another man, too. He confessed."

"Copper's nark."

"That's over now, and you have had a clean record since then. We want to help you control your urges, not to condemn what you did."

Mr Symonds looked artful. "There's nothing wrong with my mind, doctor. It's physical. I have pains and I need a doctor to examine me thoroughly." He began to undo his shirt buttons, baring his chest.

"I'll make an appointment at the hospital for you to see a physician. I can't examine you here. I am a psychiatrist and don't do physical examinations."

"I'd rather have you, doctor."

I bet you would, thought Emma grimly, but remained silent.

"Sister, I'd like you to take a sample of blood for examination. That much I can do, to eliminate certain conditions that you might have caught due to your lifestyle." Paul immersed himself in the notes while Emma swabbed the patient's arm and found a vein. She drew up blood quickly as she had a feeling that he could refuse to co-operate even when the needle was in position. She swabbed the arm again after the syringe was full.

"That was a bit quick. I wasn't ready," he said resentfully. Emma smiled. She had a memory of a man who didn't want blood taken from him and pulled the needle out when it was half in place; he'd called her a careless bitch before the very butch casualty sister took over and would have no nonsense from him.

Carefully she labelled the phial of blood and put it in a thick envelope.

"I think that's all I can do at present," Paul said. "You asked for a physical examination and we must wait until that has been done and the blood has been analysed before we think of psychiatric treatment. I must impress on you that if they prescribe drugs you must take them every day, or you could end up in real trouble."

Paul turned away, leaving Emma to make sure that

the patient had everything of his own ready to take with him. She opened the door and followed him down the stairs.

"The doctor will be here all the time now he's back from America?" he asked hopefully.

"Not all the time, but Dr Forsyth will be here and Mr Grade is due back from holiday soon. He will be in the consulting room." She thought of Paul's repugnance for the man, even though he showed no sign of it. "Dr Sykes, may be away a lot quite soon," she said. "He has to lecture in Ireland and London and maybe the States again. That's why he needed a reliable locum to take over."

Mrs Coster watched the man leave and closed the door firmly after him. "Glad none of mine turned out like him. Some can't help it, poor souls, and that's sad, but worms like him are wicked. I saw him looking at that nice picture of Rose and Mrs Miller's three that you have on the wall over there and I could have hit him."

"He thinks Paul is going away, so he might decide he doesn't want to come here again."

"What a sauce!" said Mrs Coster.

"I think he should be admitted to a psychiatric hospital for treatment, but there are tests to be checked first," Emma said. "If he turns up here on some vague excuse, I rely on you to tell him that the doctor cannot see him and if necessary ask Mick to see him in the hall."

"He needs to have his flies sewn up and a dose of bromide," Mrs Coster said cheerfully. "I'll deal with him if he shows his face here and walks over my nice clean hall tiles."

Seven

"You don't need me to tell you, but of course the powers that be will want the relevant forms filled in." The obstetrician smiled. "I don't know what happens in the Navy, but I shall recommend leave for the next six weeks until all sickness has subsided, then duty as usual until the lump becomes too uncomfortable and you have no uniform to fit you!"

Margaret picked up her clothes and went behind the screen to dress. "I wish it was me, Stella," Emma said.

"I know, but it will happen, and they say that pregnancy is catching. I'll sign a form and then Margaret can wait outside with some coffee while I take a look at you. Any trouble?"

"None as far as I know. I left off the diaphragm in America and everything is regular. Not even a bad period pain."

"Does George know his good news?"

"He's out at sea, standing by Suez, and Margaret doesn't want to worry him, but now it's definite she might tell him. She's talking of leaving the Navy and settling down in Hampshire, and I think he will urge her to do that."

"George has one child, I believe?"

76

"A boy, and Margaret is very fond of him. He will also have an adoring grandmother in the same house but in a separate flat, so he will never lack for affection and care," Emma said.

Stella gently probed Emma's flat abdomen and then washed her hands and examined her internally. "Nothing abnormal here," she said at last. "I'll write you up for some vitamins and a boost to your hormones, but only a marginal amount as you are so healthy. I have no doubt that having had one child successfully you can have another. If we stimulate your thyroid, that will urge your other hormonal glands to do their stuff."

"Thank you, Stella. I'll do what I'm told and risk being in the sick stage when we have to go to Ireland."

"North or south?"

"Both Belfast and Dublin. Paul is in great demand now and we have a new partner who can cope while he is away."

"You go with him?"

Emma nodded.

"Very wise, if you have to stay in unfamiliar hotels that have no character. I hate those places, but my husband is very good and comes with me to what must be boring congresses. Not being a medic, he likes to skive off and look at old churches, and we meet up for meals and bed."

"He's a writer, isn't he?"

"Yes, and it means he can work anywhere. As he prefers to do the first draft of a book in longhand, that's easy."

Emma sighed. "I hope to see you again soon. Rose

is getting a bit spoiled with no competition and Clive isn't a lot of help as he does what she wants most of the time – unlike Mark, Bea's youngest, who has a will of his own and was definitely boss when we were in the States."

"Go home and forget about babies. If you worry about it then it will never happen and, as one old midwife used to say, 'The fruit will grow without you shaking the tree.' I've known women who adopted and gave up all idea of having their own babies as they thought it was impossible, becoming pregnant when they were up to their eyes in adopted babies and nappies and mumps! So enjoy Ireland with Paul and bring me back some shamrocks."

Margaret already had the bloom that clings to newly pregnant women and her expression was soft. "I still can't believe it," she said as they walked from the hospital and out to Emma's car.

"Have you written to George?"

"I shall write this evening and tell him that I'm fit and well and have seen an obstetrician."

"Good. Did Stella advise antenatal exercise classes?" asked Emma. "They're becoming popular and when I had Rose I was glad to have some sort of a pattern to follow with breathing and so on." She giggled. "We were all shapes and sizes and when we were on our backs on mattresses the lumps varied from four months showing very little to positive mountains that looked ready to be delivered at any moment. Quite relaxing and it was good to know that I wasn't the only one with frequency and backache!"

"Thanks very much! I'm looking forward to the back-ache!" Margaret said with dry humour. "Where shall we have lunch? I'm starving."

"Do you want a snack or a stodgy meal?"

"At the moment I could eat a horse."

"That isn't on any menu I know about, unless you want to pop over to France! As we're nearly there we can go to the restaurant in Dickins & Jones. I hear the food is fairly good but very filling. Restaurants have a tendency to major on pies, potatoes and gooey puddings."

"Just what I need." Margaret got into the car and turned to Emma. "Thank you for taking me to see Stella. She's exactly right for her job and gave me a lot of confidence." She blushed. "In fact, I have a lot to thank you for."

"Not really," Emma said casually. "Paul and I are enjoying your visit and you're welcome at any time. Why not stay for a while until the morning sickness is over? I believe Stella suggested sick leave from the Navy, so you either stay with us where I can keep an eye on you or go back to Hampshire and have to cope alone until George comes back."

"I hate to impose on you," Margaret said.

"I haven't heard that you have close family who would help at this time. Is that right?"

"I have a stepmother who is pleasant but who wouldn't be interested in me now. She works as a secretary and I think may marry again. It's three years since my father died and she's attractive."

"No doting aunts like mine?"

"None. You're very lucky."

"It's only in the last few years that I've been aware

how much we mean to each other. When George lost Sadie, they were wonderful and we all came closer as a family. George is so fortunate to have you, Margaret. You are the rock he needs. If you hadn't come into his life he might have drifted and been very lonely." She smiled. "Aunts and cousins are useful but he needed a wife to surround him with love . . . and a family to keep Clive company."

"You might have been better at it than I shall be," Margaret said, but refused to meet Emma's eyes.

"Me and George?" Emma hoped she sounded very incredulous. "We're cousins! I fell in love with Paul and George married Sadie. George is a very nice person but not for me and I was not for him," she added firmly. "You've met my Aunt Emily?"

Margaret nodded.

"You should hear her opinion on badly matched pairs. She's usually right. She said that George and Sadie wouldn't last even if Sadie had lived, and there's never been any question of George and I coming together."

"I really thought . . ." Margaret began, but Emma interrupted her.

"I envy you, Margaret," she said. "You became pregnant soon after you were married, but I had to work at it, with Stella's help, to have Rose and now I want another baby and I have no idea if it's possible."

"Has your Aunt Emily said anything about me?" Margaret asked almost humbly.

"She approves of you, and so does Janey, and when they hear your news they'll be over the moon."

"Do you want the rest of the potatoes?" Margaret

laughed. "Do you know, I feel wonderful but still hungry. I feel I'm being accepted into a very nice family and it's a good feeling."

"I'm glad," Emma replied simply, but inwardly she was relieved to think that Margaret had lost her suspicions that George might be in love with his cousin. "Are you going to leave the Navy as soon as possible?"

Margaret took a deep breath. "The Navy has been my life ever since I left school and I shall miss it, but I want to settle down to being a wife and mother. I know George would want that too, so yes, I'll write to the Admiralty tomorrow and be free to buy civilian clothes and put my feet up when I feel tired! Such self-indulgence."

"You look different already," Emma said, laughing. "Don't go mad and buy too many dresses to fit you now, as you'll be surprised how much weight you'll put on and need to have fresh clothes all the time."

"How did you manage with clothes rationing? In uniform it was easy, as we had only to buy for holidays and off-duty, and I had friends stationed abroad who brought me gifts of dress materials from the Far East; but you had to have maternity wear as well as normal clothes that would fit you afterwards."

"Bea's father travelled to Switzerland in the diplomatic service and brought a lot of goodies back for Bea. He was very generous to me too, and Aunt Emily had material stowed away from pre-war. We made a lot of our own clothes when we were hard-up nurses in training; looking back, I'm amazed how well we looked in topcoats made from unrationed bed blankets. Lace blouses were pretty and lace with butter muslin to use as linings was off ration too. Bea had a wonderful maternity suit made from crushed velvet. Sadie saw it and wanted one like it, but she wanted everything that anyone else had and sulked if she couldn't have it."

"I'll spare George that! I don't think I'm the sulking kind, and I'm so happy, I can't wait to tell him the good news."

"Ask him to bring you a couple of kaftans from Egypt. They're fashionable now, and so much more attractive than the 'sack' dress and the other odd designs that appear in Mary Quant's Bazaar in the King's Road. You'll find them practical when you lose your waistline."

They drove back to the line of shops close to the clinic in Kensington and took their prescriptions for vitamins and Emma's mild thyroid tablets into the chemist there.

"Mick and Eileen are due back tomorrow," Emma said. "I'm curious to hear what they thought of Ireland."

Margaret went to her room to rest and Emma sorted out clothes suitable for formal dinners Paul might have to go to in Ireland and tweeds that would be useful if autumn came early, although the weather was still very warm and a prolonged summer looked likely. Rose wanted to help and was convinced that any packing meant another visit to Mark in America.

"Not this time," Emma said sadly. "I miss them as much as you do, darling, but Daddy needs us to look after him when he has to go to Ireland."

"I can go to America on the plane on my own. Mark said he went on a plane without his mummy and daddy and so could I."

"Mark sat with the pilot when Dwight took him to an air show, but they didn't fly," Emma said gently. "Mark has a great imagination. We're going to Ireland to help Daddy. If we find a leprechaun we'll bring him back with us."

"What's that?"

"A tiny little magic man with green clothes and a floppy hat. He grants wishes to good people, and plays tricks on bad ones," Emma said, smiling.

"I'm good," Rose said seriously. "I'll wish for lots of things."

"It's no good unless you ask the leprechaun, and there aren't a lot of them," Emma added hastily.

"I'll find one," Rose said firmly and Emma wished she'd never mentioned the Irish folk myth.

"Daddy, when can we go to find a leppercorn?" Rose asked as soon as she saw her father. "I want to go to Ireland *now!*"

Paul grinned. "That's one way to make her want to come with us. I thought she was hankering after Mark and the States."

"That too, but she's intrigued by little men in green who grant wishes."

"I leave you to sort this one out," he said hastily. He picked Rose up and hugged her. "We're going to Ireland next week." Paul glanced at Emma. "Everything OK?"

"Margaret will leave the Navy and get broody, and I have to tickle up my hormones."

"Good girl."

"I *am* a good girl and I want to have lots of wishes,"

Rose said complacently. She ran off to fetch her own small case and Paul kissed Emma.

"At least I don't have to go into Beattie's for another insufflation of tubes. Stella was definite about that and thinks it's only a matter of time before, as Mrs Coster would say, I 'get caught'. What an expression!"

"I'm glad you aren't as fruitful as her. What would we do with six children?"

Emma hid her face in his jacket and her voice was muffled. "We'd love them, every one."

Mick and Eileen brought Jean to see Rose as soon as they arrived home and the two girls played happily with the dolls that Eileen had bought for them until suddenly Jean rushed out and clung to Mick in tears.

"Hey, what's up?" he said, thinking the girls had quarrelled.

"It's not fair. Rose is going to Ireland and bringing back a leppercorn and she'll have lots of wishes."

"*You*'ve just come back and you have a lot of toys we bought for you over there."

"It's not a toy. He's a tiny man in a green suit and he's magic."

"Oh dear! My fault, I'm afraid. It's a joke, Jean," Emma said but knew that once Rose had an idea it would take more than magic of any kind to shift it.

"We didn't see one, but if Rose sees two she'll bring one back for you," Mick said and laughed. "There's magic enough there, sister. You'll love Ireland. Eileen's unpacking but she said she'll be ready to cook dinner as soon as you want her."

"Not this evening, Mick," Emma said firmly. "We want to hear all about your holiday. I've made pasties, and there's jelly and custard and cheese for everyone in the kitchen tonight."

"That's a relief. Eileen was knackered after the boat crossing and Jean wasn't much help as she wanted to go back to Ireland." He stared at Margaret as she came into the office, yawning. "You look like Eileen did when . . . sorry, nothing," he mumbled.

Margaret laughed. "Do all women expecting a baby have that look?" she said. "I can't keep anything private any more!"

"You really are?" Mick went pink. "Wish it was Eileen. Jean did me out of my train set so we need a boy."

"I heard that, Mick!" Eileen came into the office and smiled at Margaret. "Did I miss something?" she asked.

"Only that you're let off dinner duty as Sister wants to hear about Ireland," Mick said quickly.

"It was much nicer than I thought possible," Eileen said. "We stayed with very nice people and Jean had a good time as they love children and have a lot of their own."

"I paddled in the lake with Curran and Maeve, and picked lots of flowers," Jean said.

"I shall do that too," Rose asserted firmly, "and when I find my leppercorn he can help me."

The two girls tried to outstare each other. Eileen and Emma exchanged glances: it was becoming clear that they needed something more than each other's company, and Rose's holiday in America and Jean's

85

visit to Ireland had brought other dimensions into their lives.

"Help me to unpack the other case," Eileen suggested to Jean after they'd eaten, and she took her down to their own apartment.

"It was so easy over there," Mick said. "They take children for granted and let them have a lot of freedom but they don't seem to come to much harm as there are eyes everywhere in the villages and no real danger." He laughed. "They want to know everything about you and after the first evening they knew our names, where we came from and what we did for a living." He grinned. "They didn't ask the colour of my granny's eyes but they had everything else off pat! Complete strangers addressed us by name and asked after Jean if she wasn't with us." He shrugged. "Eileen got a bit fed up with them as they all wanted to know why she had no more children. I shut them up by saying there were medical reasons and they looked sympathetic, as if they took it for granted that Eileen wanted a big family."

"I shall say that we left the other seven at home with a nanny," Paul said.

"You'd better make that an unmarried aunt, not a nanny. They still have such angels, who stay at home and look after elderly parents and are on hand for the children."

"What if the angel wants a career?" Emma said.

"Nursing is OK, as they look to the future care of their old people, but they aren't keen on them escaping into the big city or being free to choose what they want to do."

"They could get married if they went away and met

more men," Emma said. "Most Irish girls are good-looking."

"The men tend to marry late over there. They have to find work and earn enough to support a family and there aren't that many jobs going. As soon as they have a good job they may marry but they are afraid of too many babies arriving, and with no birth control allowed that is a problem."

"It isn't just the Irish who use unmarried aunts and sisters." Emma frowned. "I know that Aunt Emily is only half Irish but her Victorian parents had the same conviction, that the youngest unmarried girl stayed at home and looked after the parents and the home. In Emily's case they had a shop that kept her busy, but she did have a sweetheart. She dared not break away and marry him." She shrugged. "He died in the First World War but she was almost content as she was close to her mother and her brothers and sisters."

"She never shows any sign of being embittered by that," Paul said. "If all my patients who grumble about the 'might have been' could see her, they might be ashamed."

"Life *was* hard, even in families who had enough to live on," Emma added. "It taught them to cut their losses and count their blessings."

Paul began to clear away the dishes. "You can count your blessings that I don't ask you to help wash up, Mick. Go on, off to bed and get some sleep. You are all panda-eyed."

Eight

"I think Eileen was glad to see us leave," Emma remarked. "She loves her job as housekeeper and coped so well while we were in America that I feel an intruder in my own kitchen."

"It's not really a problem, is it?" Paul asked rather anxiously.

"No." Emma tried to sound convincing. The last few days had been so full of packing, and seeing even more friends who wanted to meet and hear about Bea and America, that there had been no time for friendly chats over cups of tea. And Eileen was having trouble with Jean, who had been so enchanted with Ireland and the many friends she made there that she was now slightly sulky. She annoyed everyone, including Rose, with her boasting.

"Nearly there," Paul said, and Emma saw masts appearing over the tops of the buildings by the quay and heard a ship's siren through the morning mist. It was so familiar, and the sea was as blue as it was in Cowes Roads. Rose stirred and sat up after sleeping through the train journey from Swansea to the docks. "It was a bit of an early start for you, Rose, but at least you'll be wide awake when we're on the ferry."

"The boats aren't as big as the one we went on to go to America," Rose said in a self-satisfied tone. "Jean said she went to Ireland in a big, big boat but these are little."

"We went on a liner. That's different. These are very big as far as ferries go and you mustn't compare the two." Paul spoke sharply, as he had noticed a growing-apart of the two little girls and hated the thought of dissension between the two families who depended so much on each other.

"Jean said she put money into a machine and chocolate came out," Rose said and looked hopeful.

"We'll see if there is one as soon as we're on board," Emma said. "What else have we to do to keep up with Miss Jean?"

"She showed me her name on a piece of metal. The machine stamped the letters that her daddy picked out and it said 'Jean Grade' but there weren't enough letters for the money they put in to spell out where she lives."

"I remember that from when I was at school. I thought they'd all gone," Emma said. "Unless I held on to the letter I wanted the arm jumped, and I had some very strange messages from the ones on the Portsmouth ferry. I kept one for ages that spelled out 'Emma Jexa' and I never did get one right."

"The wonders of modern science," Paul said solemnly. "Here we are and I'm glad that we sent the main luggage in advance as I see no porters who look strong enough to carry it! No, Rose, we carry our own hand luggage and yours isn't very heavy, so come on and don't hold up the people behind us."

Emma raised her eyebrows. It wasn't often that Paul spoke so sternly to his daughter, but she saw that it might be necessary if Rose was not to rule the family as Jean seemed to do with Eileen and Mick.

The crossing was calm and the sun broke through early cloud to shine on the water and bring warmth to the passengers reclining on the steamer loungers. Rose found the machine that gave out small thin bars of Nestlé milk chocolate for a penny a time and was allowed to eat one as there was so little in the packet.

The name-printing machine had a line of children waiting to use it and Rose was impatient. "When is it my turn?" she asked, and Emma recognised the whining element that Jean now used to great effect with her mother Eileen.

"There isn't going to be a turn if you speak to me like that," Emma said. "If there are people before you then wait your turn politely and be quiet." Rose lapsed into moody silence and went to look over the rail at the creamy wake from the stern of the ferry.

"It's nearly lunchtime," Paul said tactfully, and Rose had to abandon the printing and follow him.

"Cheer up," Emma said softly. "We'll be on this boat for hours and when we have finished lunch I expect there will be very few children round that machine."

"Promise?"

"No, I can't promise that, as what happens on the boat has nothing to do with me," Emma replied. "There are lots of children on the boat who want to be first in everything just like you, but we must wait our turn."

"But I want . . ."

"I remember someone saying to me when I was a little girl, 'You want and make a fuss, then you must go on wanting. Wait or go without!' I learned that I wasn't the only important person in the world," she added, but smiled as she recalled the agony of a four-year-old's frustrated wishes. "I know it's hard to wait but there will be lots of lovely things to do when we get to Dublin and you'll make friends just as Jean did."

"I want to see my leppercorn," Rose said. "Jean didn't see one."

"Mark has never seen one, nor have Avril and Johnnie, so does it really matter if you don't see one either?" asked Paul.

"They didn't have leppercorns in America," Rose said in a superior voice.

"No, but they had a lot of other things and you were very happy with what you had," Paul told her.

"I miss Mark," Rose began and the corners of her mouth turned down.

"So do we. We miss America and Bea and Dwight and the children and I miss American pizzas," Paul said.

"Come on, Rose, don't just stand there looking at that poster," Emma said. "I'm hungry. I hope there are some good things on the menu."

Paul grinned. "Talk your way out of this one," he said to Emma.

"Oh, *no!*" Emma burst out laughing and Rose looked

triumphant. The poster showed an Irish beauty spot with a signpost in the foreground. Rose couldn't read the sign that said LEPRECHAUN CROSSING but she could see the picture of a little man in green, wearing a floppy hat and a wicked smile.

"That's where he lives," Rose asserted. "I want . . . please may I go there?" she asked more politely as if to make sure her parents would agree with her.

"That place is in Kerry, a lot further on from Dublin," Paul explained. "However, we shall be going to a lot of villages where they may have signposts like that, so we might find another later."

Rose giggled. "It shows there are lots of leppercorns and we can find them and take some home."

"That signpost only means that you must wait and look both ways before you cross the road," Paul said. "It doesn't mean there are real leprechauns there. I'm afraid you'll be disappointed; they're only like fairies in books, and don't really exist."

"I shall find them," Rose asserted rather grandly, as if her father was not quite as clever as he thought.

"Good! You can look for them and let us know when you find one," Paul answered. "It will give you something to do when we're in the car on long journeys. Better than I Spy."

Rose unpeeled the foil from the tiny portion of butter and put butter on her roll. "How did you know that was butter?" Emma asked.

"Jean told me."

Emma sighed. Was the whole journey to and stay

in Ireland to be an echo of what Jean Grade had seen and done?

"Can I have another penny for chocolate? Will there be many children waiting to print their names?" Rose asked hopefully as soon as she finished eating.

To Emma's relief, the printing machine was old and cumbersome and out of true and Rose found it boring after the first two efforts. Her chocolate bar was broken in half and gradually Jean was mentioned less as the expected results of everything she had boasted about were cut down to size and no longer impressed Rose. Soon she was more like her usual cheerful self.

A taxi took them to a pretty hotel where they were to stay the night. It was by the shore, with a path that led down to a small beach, and Emma wished they could stay for a few days before going on in a hired car to Dublin. But Rose made the most of what time they had there as she found a swing hanging from a tree in the garden; while Emma and Paul sat on a rustic bench and drank in the view over the harbour, Rose was completely absorbed.

"I didn't realise that Mick looked so Irish until we came here. The hotel manager looks very like him but Mick's cockney voice isn't like his."

"The elderly lady over there has a bit of Emily about her, and I'm sure we shall see faces that are half familiar all the time we're here."

"I haven't seen anyone as lovely as you," Paul said, "but after seeing the picture of your grandmother, I do see traces of her in certain faces here, and Emily swears you are like her."

93

"Somehow it seems familiar. I know it's only because I'm expecting to feel a kind of kinship, but I love the deep green of the meadows and the fact that the sea is over there."

Rose swung slowly and hummed to herself as she'd done when she was a baby and was tired. "Bed for you, Rose," Emma said firmly. "The bath is huge and there are a lot of packets of soap and shampoo that we can use."

"Are they ours?"

"Yes; most hotels have them now."

"Can I take them home if we don't use them?"

"I suppose you can, but there will be packets of soap in the other hotels," Emma said. "I have soap and shampoo in my bag if there's none in the other bathrooms so you needn't collect these."

"Please. I want to take some back for Jean," Rose said self-righteously, then added maliciously, "She didn't stay in proper hotels. They stayed in ordinary houses with other people."

"I was very impressed when Mick told me about the lovely people they met," Paul said. "I almost changed our plans as it sounded far more warm and homely to stay on farms and in private houses with families."

Rose set her jaw, annoyed at having her one-upmanship spoiled. "I shall take the soap home," she said firmly. "Jean didn't have free soap."

"We'll collect all we can," Paul said. "It will be useful in the handbasins of the patients' lavatories. Personally, I shall use our own while we're here as I don't think the hotel soap is very good."

Emma tried not to laugh and took Rose to have her bath. She tucked her into the small bed in the alcove at the side of the main bedroom after giving her fresh milk, biscuits and a banana.

Paul was waiting by the dining-room door. "I asked the girl in reception if someone could listen outside our room at intervals in case Rose was awake, but I think she's so tired that she'll sleep the clock round. I'm hungry and we deserve some wine with our meal."

Emma smiled. "I really do miss Mark," she said. "It takes one bossy child to manage another. Rose needs him."

"Rose needs a brother or sister of her own, but she'll have to be patient, as we are. It will happen. I have faith in nature and Stella, in that order."

"We'll have coffee in the bar," Paul said after the meal. "I have some notes I should glance at and I can do that there." He sighed. "A flask of wine, good food and you is paradise," he misquoted, "but Dublin looms up and I must be ready tomorrow. I'm being very selfish, bringing you over here while I work, but it does make all the difference to see you, touch you and share the good and bad bits with you."

"I wouldn't miss it. I was ready to come away again. Rose and I can sightsee while you give lectures and we can meet different people in the evenings."

Paul laughed. "You have a very important task. You're responsible for leprechauns."

"Don't remind me. I want to forget little green men this evening." They walked out through the main entrance to breathe the warm evening air and the smell of night-scented stocks came to them, sweet and nostalgic. "Aunt Emily grows them," Emma remembered, and suddenly her aunt felt close. A dampness in the air made them go back into the bar and a man smiled as he entered the hotel, droplets of fine dew on his jacket. "Sure it's going to be a soft night, God be praised," he said in a low voice, and Emma knew that she was in Ireland, among the people from whom her grandmother came.

Breakfast was a big meal with bacon and eggs and fruit. The waitress put a small breadboard on the table with a warm loaf on it.

Rose eyed the bread with concern. "It's a funny shape, Mummy."

"It's Irish soda bread. Aunt Emily makes it sometimes for Aunt Janey. I've tasted it and it's very good." Emma cut a thick slice that included one of the points of crust rising from the cross-cut loaf, and then cut it in half. Rose piled butter on her piece and added strawberry jam. "Why don't we have this at home?" she said through a mouthful of warm crumbs.

"I'll make some when we go back, but it doesn't keep well. It has to be freshly made and I haven't time to make it often." She laughed. "That's one very nice thing that Jean had when they were here. The farmer's wife gave Eileen a good recipe, so we'll all have some."

"I wish we were staying on a farm," Rose said.

"And not have free soap?" Paul asked. "Eat up, we're

ready to leave in half an hour and it's a long drive to Dublin."

"Are there any leppercorns in Dublin?"

"I have no idea, but before we leave here you could buy a postcard with a picture of a leprechaun on it."

"I want . . ." Rose began, but her parents ignored her until she smiled, put her hand in Paul's and asked sweetly, "Please Daddy may I buy one for Jean as well?"

Emma looked pleased and Paul hurried with Rose to the stand full of lurid picture postcards. "Hurry up," he said. "Those are the ones you need." He paid for the cards and managed to move Rose away from the pictures of Irish dancing and some vulgar cards with even more vulgar captions.

"But Daddy, can't I have that one? He looks just like Mario down the road from us and I'm sure he'd like that card."

"I don't think so," Paul said hastily and wondered what Mario would think of the awful picture and unflattering words. "Mario is Italian, not Irish, and he wouldn't understand."

They put the luggage into the car boot. "It's good not to have to depend on taxis and buses," Emma said. She gave Rose a picture book and told her that she would have to amuse herself for a while. "When you've looked at your book you can watch for leprechauns and girls in green and red cloaks like the dancers on the cards."

Cows stood in deep pastures, cottage gardens were bright with late-summer flowers, and a lad with red hair on a rough-coated pony gave way to the car in a country lane. "He isn't riding on a saddle," Rose said. She turned round to stare at him as the car accelerated and the boy grinned. "Why doesn't he fall off?"

"He probably rides like that every day and is used to it," Paul said.

"Mark fell off when he did that," Rose told him, "and Auntie Bea said it served him right if he was hurt. Does that boy live on a farm? I like that horse. Can I have a ride?"

"Not without a saddle, and you'd find an English saddle very different from the ones you had in America."

"Do all the boys in Ireland ride like he does? Perhaps there aren't any saddles in Ireland."

"Only farm boys and gypsies who have been with horses all their lives ride like that," Emma said.

Paul slowed the car and wound a window open. The smell of horses came in on a whiff of cooking and Rose gazed entranced at a group of gypsy wagons on the wide verge, with the haltered horses cropping the grass. "We'll see a lot of those," Paul said and drove on in spite of Rose's plaintive cries to him to let her smooth the horses.

"Auntie Bea told me that the Irish love horses and have a lot of beautiful racing stables. Maybe we can see one when Daddy is busy, or there might be a riding school that you can go to later. Her father knows a lot about racehorses and he said he's going to buy one."

"Will he let me ride it?" Rose asked.

"He'll have a real jockey to ride it. He doesn't ride and I doubt if he could manage an energetic horse," Emma pointed out. She was amused at the idea of Bea's rather solid and sophisticated-looking father riding anything less comfortable than a smooth limousine.

"Why does he want a horse if someone else is going to ride it? When I have a horse of my very own, I shall ride it," Rose said.

"I don't think Jean went riding over here, so it isn't certain that you can find somewhere to hire a horse," Paul pointed out.

Rose looked surprised. "Jean doesn't like horses. She said there were two on the farm where they stayed and one tried to lick her and she cried."

"I thought she liked animals," Emma said. "She has lots of cuddly toys like rabbits and kittens."

"She doesn't like real ones. Her mummy makes the toys but said she is glad that Jean doesn't like pets."

"I remember that Eileen wouldn't take Jean to the zoo," Emma recalled. "Mick took her but they came back after only half an hour because Jean was frightened of the monkeys."

"Two little girls being brought up under the same roof, even if they are in separate apartments, are becoming so different," Paul said quietly while Rose became engrossed in her picture book.

"I think that Bea's family influenced Rose in America but I noticed even before we went there that the two girls often played with very different toys. When they go to school next year they'll make other friends and we shall see further changes." Emma frowned. "I am very fond of Jean, but when she comes back from playing with Betty, she says spiteful things, and last week she had a nasty bruise on her arm where she'd been slapped."

"I know that Eileen has a friend and goes to her house once a week," Paul said. "Mick isn't all that keen and refuses to invite her to the flat, but Eileen says she makes her laugh. I know very little about her."

"Eileen's friend has three small children including Betty and they are a bit wild. Betty is the same age as Jean and younger than her brother and sister who I think bully her. Eileen was cross about the bruise but couldn't find out who'd done it. She decided that it was an accident, but when Mick insisted on knowing what had happened and asked Jean, she said that it was Jack who hit her and told her she mustn't tell anyone, or, to use his own words, she'd get another one."

"Nice child," Paul said drily. "Which one of that family do I see first in the clinic? Was that why Mick was laying down the law to Eileen?"

"She wouldn't tell me, but I'm sure that was what caused the tension. I expect it will be sorted out by the time we get back," Emma said. "I'm going to forget about them all now, and enjoy Ireland."

Nine

"This is more convenient, as we are close to the university, but I enjoyed the Meadow Lane Hotel," Paul said.

"Endless corridors where I shall get lost and a more impersonal staff," Emma decided, and sounded uncertain. "I suppose there's a lot more to do here and Dublin *is* a beautiful city, but Rose was happy with the swing and trying to find crabs under the seaweed on the beach."

"And you? I feel guilty when I think you're bored."

"Paul darling, I am not bored," Emma said firmly. "I want us all to find what we need to do and to enjoy it. You have a lecture to give, but we can explore Dublin and every time you're busy, Rose and I will be happy going on one of the many trips that seem to be available. I never thought I'd look forward to being a real tourist, as on the island we rather stood back and looked at visitors as strange creatures who had no part in our lives, but here I shall become a culture vulture like the average American matron and see everything."

"You'll be looking for leprechauns, and I doubt if Dublin is true leprechaun country."

"Don't remind me. I think we are over that hurdle

as Rose saw some dolls in the showcase in the foyer and among the dancing girls there were two small dolls dressed as you know what! We spent ten minutes wondering if they were really dolls or just sleeping."

"I hope this isn't developing into an obsession," Paul said seriously.

"I don't think she needs a shrink just yet, and I believe she's convinced now that leprechauns are only in the imagination. It was a bit sad when she decided that the ones in the showcase were dolls."

"It isn't just the leprechauns. Her general attitude with Jean isn't as good as it was and each one wishes to do everything better than the other and to crow about it. They're definitely not as close as they were."

"Rose was determined to find a leprechaun, and believed that they are real and are here in Ireland for her to find," Emma said. "It's hard to have your dreams shattered, but as yet she hasn't cried over them as she still hopes that I'm wrong. Do you recall the floods of tears when someone told Jean there was no Santa Claus, and Jean told Rose and they both had a good cry?"

"I think I'll buy a couple of the dolls and hide them in the luggage. One each when we get back will smooth the way for Jean to be a part of Rose's fantasy," Paul said.

Emma reached up to kiss him. "You look terribly formal," she said, laughing. "Your audience will be very impressed."

"I wish I was coming with you. They want me there for lunch so it will be almost dinnertime when I get back."

"You'll love it, and we shall have a ball looking in every souvenir shop that Rose sees. I have a
built-in nostalgia for trashy memorabilia, so it isn't all
for Rose!"

"Rather you than me – and I don't want a joke glass
that spills Guinness over me when I try to drink it."

"I promise. What about boxer shorts with shamrocks
all over them?"

"That will do for Mick."

She watched him stride away and knew that he was
already concentrating on the work ahead, but when
Rose insisted on going down to the foyer to see her
"leppercorn" dolls, the girl serving in the kiosk shook
her head and told Rose that a gentleman had already
bought both of them and she had parcelled them up
to be collected later. Emma smiled tenderly. He'd
remembered, even though his mind was full of his
lecture about battle fatigue.

"We'll see if there are any more in the shops," Emma
promised, but added gently when she saw that Rose was
upset, "They really are only dolls, Rose. They aren't
real and you will see a lot of them, I'm sure."

The tourist map of Dublin suggested many interesting places to visit, but it was enough to wander
from the hotel into the main part of the city and
just look at the lovely streets and the inviting shops.
Emma was reminded that the historic buildings in
Dublin hadn't suffered during the war, since southern
Ireland was neutral. The soft sunlight cast a warm
glow over the old, untouched stones. The late-night
shower had washed the leaves of the trees lining the

main thoroughfare, leaving them glistening and turning in the morning breeze. She wanted to turn to Paul or Bea to share everything and felt a tinge of sadness, but Rose dragged at her hand to show her a shop that sold Irish linen embroidered with shamrocks and tiny figures of dancing girls in red and green.

"There aren't any leppercorns," she said disconsolately.

"I want to buy something for Aunt Emily, Aunt Janey and Eileen, so you must help me choose," Emma said.

Rose relaxed and suggested a lot of unsuitable gifts.

"We can't buy them now as we might see something we like better," Emma pointed out, and put back a luridly decorated crinoline lady destined to cover some unlucky person's telephone.

"Eileen would like that," Rose said, and Emma was inclined to agree, but they moved on and by lunchtime were tired and hungry.

Music from a pub almost convinced Emma that they could eat there but she was shy of going anywhere unfamiliar like that without a male escort. It's not unlike London, she thought. There must be areas such as the ones she knew where unaccompanied women could or could not eat in safety. They settled for a department-store restaurant and ate fish and chips and ice cream, which suited Rose but was uninteresting. The steady buzz of Irish voices was everywhere and Emma doubted if the Irish really needed to kiss the Blarney Stone to give them the gift of eloquence, as they seemed to talk even when they were eating.

A feeling that she was missing something was unsettling. She watched and listened but was on the fringe, apart from what was being discussed, and the intimate laughter was beguiling but not for her. It was full of English-speaking Irish voices and yet was foreign. I'm expecting too much, she decided. I came here wanting to feel at home because of Aunt Emily and the family but I am an alien.

Rose was tired; they returned to the hotel so that she could have a nap, and Emma was free to explore the hotel and the garden. The boutique was similar to the ones in American hotels, full of extravagant clothes and costume jewellery, and the music from muted speakers was featureless and bland. Emma bought a magazine and a paperback novel and wished they had been able to stay in a smaller hotel or on a farm as Mick and his family had done.

The tailored gardens were like a public park and the sound of traffic came through the high hedges, loud enough to make sitting on a bench impossible. A hint of panic threatened to overcome her usual good humour. Was every day here going to be as boring? She sat in the lounge and firmly opened her paperback, then ordered tea to be served in half an hour after she had brought Rose down from her sleep.

"Where are we going now, Mummy?"

"We're going to have tea and wait for Daddy."

"I want something to do."

"So do I!" Emma laughed. It was a relief to know

that they were both bored in a wonderful city where life throbbed and there was so much to see. "We'll go down to the shop on the corner again and buy a jigsaw puzzle."

To Emma's relief there was no sign of leprechauns on the pictures showing the finished puzzles and they bought one with fairies, toads and rabbits.

"My my, you do look busy," Paul said when he arrived far earlier than expected. He grinned. "Is that the best entertainment that Dublin's fair city can offer?"

"All the trips were too long for Rose, and we've explored so many shops that I have shopper's indigestion! We bought nothing but one jigsaw and we had lunch in a very dull store and tea here."

"Great! I did rather better. We had a light lunch and I sampled real Irish Guinness, which was good."

"Lucky you," Emma replied without enthusiasm.

"We also have an invitation to dinner tonight in a real Irish home."

"But surely we can't leave the hotel?" Emma said with a glance at Rose, who was trying to force a piece of jigsaw into the wrong place.

"I hope you don't object to leaving this wonderful palace?"

Emma looked surprised but rather pleased. "We aren't going *home*? Didn't they enjoy your lecture?"

"As Dwight would say, I wowed them and they begged for more. I met a professor who was in Harvard when I was there and he was keen for us to visit them when we came to Ireland, but I dismissed it as one of those invitations that says politely that we'd be welcome if we were passing but they might be at a loss if we turned up unexpectedly."

"Does he know of a better hotel? Is that where we're going to dinner tonight – once we've solved one small problem?"

"Rose? No problem. She comes too, and we all stay with them just outside Dublin."

"Stay with them?"

"Close your mouth, dear. Is that expression one of amazement or dread?"

"Spell it out in words of one syllable for my poor little brain," she suggested caustically, but her eyes glinted and she felt happier than she had done all day.

Paul hugged her. "You must have been bored! You haven't asked me if they're pleasant or house-trained or if they live in a tent."

"So long as it's a big tent, I'll change for that," she said with feeling. "This is a sad place, Paul, the kind of hotel that takes only people passing through, and I saw nobody I wanted to chat to as most of the guests are men alone or older couples without children who are booked every day on tours."

"Poor darling. I know exactly what you mean, and I felt guilty leaving you. Think what it's like to be a man alone here, and even worse for a woman who can't go out to the pubs on her own."

"You are serious? We *are* moving to stay with them? Tell me a bit about them."

"Michael O'Dwyer is a professor of anthropology who was in the States studying ethnic tribes of Indians. He's attached to the University of Dublin where his main work is with Romany gypsies. Remember, we saw a camp on our way here. He is fascinated by their old customs and ways of life."

"We have a few genuine Romany families at home – Aunt Emily knew a family when she was a child. She says they are not like the tinkers who say they are gypsies. The ones she met were honest, very wise and proud of their heritage."

Paul laughed. "I can see that you'll have a lot in common with Michael, as you have a witch for an aunt who tells the future. Are you sure Emily isn't a foundling left by the gypsies?"

"Is there a Mrs O'Dwyer?"

"Nuala, a real Irish name. I met her once at Harvard, and she's very nice."

"Nice? Does that mean a homely body who knits, or is she too glamorous for you to admit that she's pretty?" Emma teased.

"Very pretty and a busy lady like you."

"Children?" Emma glanced at Rose, who seemed to be oblivious to their conversation.

"Three, including the youngest, a boy of six."

Rose looked up. "Is his name Mark?"

"No, it's Liam."

"Isn't this an imposition? Do we stay for a day or so and then have to find another hotel?"

"No, they insist on our becoming part of the family for as long as we're here."

"Do you think they'll like us?"

"We'll soon find out. Pack everything and I'll check out of the hotel and collect some things from the foyer."

Paul grinned. "You'll have to ask Liam if he's ever met a leprechaun, Rose."

"Mummy says they're not real and I shall never find one but you never know," she whispered in a conspiratorial voice. "Where are we going?" Rose crammed her book in with her clothes and picked up the pieces of jigsaw to put in the box. "I might let Liam do some of this," she said in a lofty tone.

"You're going to stay with a family who have been kind enough to invite us. We don't know them and you must be on your best behaviour. Liam might feel too old to play with you, so be careful what you say to him."

Rose saw that her mother was serious and nodded. "I want to go there. I don't like this hotel."

"Everything ready?" said Paul half an hour later.

"Everything, including the soap that Rose insisted on taking for Jean."

"I'll ask the porter to bring the bags down to the car," Paul said.

"I still have no idea where we're going," Emma said. "I feel that we're being kidnapped." She hugged Rose and they giggled.

"That's better. I thought you'd given up laughing," Paul said. "If this invitation hadn't come we'd have had to rent an apartment to feel more at home. I'm always amazed how a house or a hotel affects me and I know it does for you. I walk into Aunt Emily's house and feel warm and wanted but that place," he added with an exaggerated shudder, "makes me feel there are skeletons in the cupboard."

"Watch it! This little jug has big ears," Emma pointed out as she saw Rose becoming interested in the conversation. "Look, Rose! What a big dog."

"I didn't see it."

"We'll see another soon. We seem to be heading away from the city."

Industrial buildings gave way to sparse groups of suburban villas and then a patch of open country. Paul stopped the car to consult a map and Emma suggested that he ask someone the way.

"Michael said a map would be better. If you ask an Irishman for directions he'll tell you in detail. Even if he has no idea where a place is he'll want to be obliging, even if he sends you in the wrong direction! I'll follow this side road and we should see the house in five minutes."

A high fence ran along the side of the lane and a thatch-roofed lich-gate opened on to a driveway leading to a large house of ochre stone. The porch door was open and a woman sat on the side seat sorting eggs into two baskets. "She's like Mrs Caws who has the hens on the island," whispered Rose.

Carefully the baskets were set on the ground and Emma smiled at the dark-haired girl who stood up to greet them.

"I'm Mary, the nanny, but you'd never guess it. I fetch eggs and go to market and make bread and sometimes even look after the children! Come in while I find Herself."

Paul smiled. "How's this for atmosphere?"

Rose ran ahead into the dim hall and stared at

110

the embroidered hangings on the stone walls. A long refectory table was covered with a dark woven cloth and on it were ceramic dishes that Paul thought must be very old. "It's like a film set," Emma murmured. "Look up there! It's a minstrels' gallery."

A pretty woman in blue trousers and a man's shirt of bright green came into the room. "It's good to see you," she assured them. "I've been anxious to meet Emma and Rose, and I remember Paul with pleasure from Harvard."

Her voice was warm and lilting and her laugh welcoming. "I won't shake hands as I've just mucked out the animals. I'll tidy up and leave you with Mary to find your rooms." She glanced at the wall clock. "Drinks in half an hour and dinner to follow, but don't bother to change."

"Where are the children?" asked Rose.

"They're doing their chores," Mary said. "Sure you'll see enough of the rascals, but if they want to keep rabbits then they have to clean the hutches and feed them. If they don't put them in the hutches at night the fox might get them."

Rose smiled. "I like it here."

Emma picked up a case and followed Paul and Mary up the sweeping stairs. She noticed that Rose carried her own case and her jacket without being told to, and that her face was wreathed in smiles.

A slackening of tension in the comfortable bedroom and the fact that Rose accepted that she would sleep in a small adjoining room alone was reassuring, and the view from the windows of farmland and horses was a far cry from Dublin's streets. A box of shabby toys and a pile of well-thumbed books in the small bedroom took Rose's attention and she was reluctant to go down to dinner.

"Come on, Rose. You haven't met the children," Emma said, and wondered if the family all ate together or if the children ate with the nanny as they did in the evenings in America when the Sykeses had stayed with Bea and Dwight.

Mary was waiting at the foot of the stairs. "Ah, there you are! Aren't you the punctual ones!" She led the way into a large living room where drinks were set out on a low table with crystal glasses and fine bone-china dishes full of crisps and nuts. More solid glasses were full of orange juice for the children and Rose was suddenly shy as a bigger girl offered her a crisp.

"I'm Tara and this is Patrick. He's the oldest and the bossiest," she said. "Liam is having to change his shirt as he smells of horses," she added cheerfully.

"I'm Rose and I don't have any brothers or sisters."

"I wish I was called Rose," Tara said. "It's so pretty."

Patrick gave a derisive snort. "You couldn't be called Rose. You should see her after she's cleaned the rabbits. Pooh!"

"Patrick!" Nuala sounded firm but didn't raise her voice and she was smiling. "Make yourself useful and fetch Liam if his fingernails are clean. Myra will be wanting us sitting down in five minutes. Michael, you're on time for once," she said cheerfully as a tall man with light brown hair and freckles greeted

Paul with enthusiasm and turned to smile at Emma and Rose.

"I don't know how to thank you," Emma began.

"Then don't try. I know that hotel and it lets Dublin down," said Nuala. "We'll visit some of the better sights in the city and you'll forget your first impression. In any case, we wanted to have you here and we like people."

Emma turned to look at the small hurricane that came through the doorway, followed closely by Patrick. "I *did* wash my hands," Liam said. "He made me do them again with a brush and I got all wet!" Paul glanced across at his wife and they both laughed. Liam was small for his age and his manner was so like Mark Miller's that it was amusing.

Rose was entranced and wide-eyed as she listened to the family teasing as they sat down to dinner. Tara sat with Rose and the boys were separated by their parents and Mary, who ate with them. The food was well cooked and appetising but simple: Irish stew, mashed potatoes and green vegetables, soda bread and butter and local cheeses, ice cream and stewed fruit.

"We'll have coffee once the children are upstairs," Nuala said, and Mary took Rose by the hand and led her away with the others. "You can go up to say good-night to Rose later," Nuala went on. "She'll be fine, just fine with Mary and Tara."

Ten

Emma woke to a fine day and Paul humming softly as he came out of the shower. "Your face is cold," she said sleepily when he bent over the bed to kiss her.

"Wake up, lazy-bones. Breakfast as soon as you've showered and dressed."

"I'd better see Rose first. She was fast asleep when I came up to say good-night."

"Too late. Tara helped her dress half an hour ago and they're in the garden."

"Ever felt unwanted?" Emma smiled. "I still can't believe this is happening. Everything is so casual, and yet it's all organised and in many ways very disciplined."

Paul held her hands and pulled her from the bed. He held her close, her body soft and as yielding as it had been last night when they made love. "Get dressed before I seduce you," Paul said huskily.

"Again?" she asked and escaped into the shower room.

"The children have had breakfast," Mary said later when Emma joined Paul downstairs. "Liam wanted to show Rose his rabbits and Patrick's gone along to his friend next door to exercise the ponies. I'll make more coffee as Nuala said she'll join you for breakfast."

"Tara seems to like younger children," Emma said. "Is she always as good with them as she was with Rose last night?"

"I think you ought to know." Mary looked back at the doorway to make sure she wasn't overheard. "Tara has a small problem. Sure it's nothing at all, but she loves children a little too much for her age. She's protective of them because her mother lost a child of one year and Tara has not forgotten." She paused, and seemed on the point of tears. "It was a little boy, and we all loved him. I came here to be nanny to the family when Liam was born and when the baby was expected I was kept on here, but he died of meningitis the week after his first birthday and it made us all sad, God help us."

"How terrible." Emma was shocked: her impression of Nuala was of a calm, happy mother with no tragedy in her background.

"It's been said now, and she will not talk of it to anyone, but you have to know as you have Rose and Tara can be possessive at times."

"Thank you for telling me."

"We fill her time with the animals and she likes school and the nuns who teach her, but there are times when she stops eating and mopes and wants only her dolls."

"This seems such a happy home."

"It is that. Make no mistake, we are all happy here and Tara is very fond of the horses, so she will give her love to them."

"I have a good breakfast because I often forget to eat lunch," Nuala said as she sat down and they began to eat the eggs and bacon that Myra put before them. "Michael had to leave early as he has students today and you have a lecture to give this afternoon, Paul, don't you?"

"Less fraught than yesterday but of value, I think. I was asked to include a talk on child psychology so that's what I'm talking about today." He avoided looking directly at Nuala but Emma noticed that she was suddenly tense. "Emma sometimes sits in on my lectures as it helps in our clinics if she knows the score."

Emma remained silent. It had been a long time since she had listened to one of the lectures, and she wondered why he mentioned it now.

"Could I come to hear you?" Nuala looked at Emma. "Could we both go, and leave the children to Mary?"

"Of course. I want to see what the university is like inside and Rose seems very happy with Tara and Liam."

"Rose is very self-contained and confident," Nuala said. "I was glad to see that Liam won't have everything his own way there. She doesn't mind saying what she thinks."

"Our housekeeper has a little girl and she and Rose play together but they have separate lives," Paul said. "America was an education for Rose as she had three lively children in the Miller family who were just what she needed. Liam is like Mark, who she adored."

"I'm glad she prefers Liam to Tara. I noticed Rose shrugged away from Tara when she tried to lift her up as if she was a baby."

"Tara is so sweet with her," Emma replied. "But after America and lovely naughty little Mark and her big cousin Clive who has been staying with us in London, she prefers boys. She'll be a tomboy if we don't civilise her!"

Nuala smiled and seemed pleased. "Come down to the paddock and meet Kavanagh and Sligo. I think Rose might be there now."

The broad field was roughly mown but full of thistles and Emma was glad to be wearing flat shoes that covered her feet well. Clumps of fading field daisies and trampled buttercups showed where animals had moved about the area and on the far side were two donkeys held on halters by Rose and Liam.

"Look, Mummy! Sligo is just like the donkey at the stables in Washington."

"Be careful. Remember that Mark was butted when he slapped him and annoyed him."

Rose laughed. "Liam said Sligo kicks, so I stay by his head."

Tara sat on a log and looked disapproving. She held two dolls on her lap and watched the children, but when Liam slipped on the moist grass she ignored him; he sat up and rubbed his bruised leg as if it hurt. Nuala ran forward to pick up the rope that he had dropped and to see that no real harm had been done.

"He's showing off, Ma," Tara said. "He thinks Rose wants to play with smelly donkeys, when I have my nice babies to show her."

"Babies?" Rose stared at her. "Those are dolls." She looked at Tara indulgently. "At the hotel I saw some leppercorns and thought they were real but Mummy said they were only dolls, and so are those." She sighed deeply. "I wish they *were* real. I want to have a leppercorn

117

of my very own; a real one with green clothes and a funny hat and he'll give me wishes if I'm good."

Tara snatched up her dolls and stamped her foot. "Leprechauns are wicked. They took away my baby brother and if I see one I'll kill him!"

Paul sat on the log and looked up at her and Nuala turned pale. Tara saw the calm face and sympathetic eyes and moved closer to him. "How do you know?" he asked.

"My baby brother was in bed and they came and took him away and he never came back."

"Did you see them?"

Tara stared at him as if he wanted her to tell a lie. "They came," she insisted.

"You saw them?"

"No, they don't let many people see them," she said.

Rose was puzzled. "I've seen pictures of leppercorns and you *can* see them on the pictures so there must have been some at some time. How can I have one of my own if I can't see him?" Paul paused while Rose's logic seeped in. "How do you know it was a leppercorn if you didn't see him? They give wishes and are kind, unless you're naughty, and I am a good girl," Rose added piously. "Were you very naughty?" she said as an afterthought.

"No, I was good and the leprechauns were bad," Tara said passionately. "Bad, bad, bad!"

Rose looked abashed at the outburst and backed away, finding comfort in the rough warm coat of the donkey; Emma held her hand.

"If you didn't see the leprechauns, who told you they'd taken your baby away?" Paul asked seriously.

Tara eyed him rebelliously but refused to answer, and Nuala whisered to Emma that this was what happened every time they mentioned the baby.

"Did you dream that a little man in green clothes took away your baby?"

"No, I had no dream," Tara admitted.

"Then someone must have talked about it and told you what happened."

"I think you're silly," Rose said. "My mummy said they're like fairies and if you believe in them they are kind unless you do wrong and I shall find one and take him home to give me wishes. They don't steal babies," she added scornfully. "I expect the lady leppercorns have babies of their own."

"Come on, Rose, let's run with the donkeys to the hedge over there," Liam said. "I bet I can run faster than you. And when the donkeys are tired, Patrick will put them to the bridle and we can ride them."

Rose pulled on the halter and Sligo reluctantly followed her. "I still think you're silly, Tara," she called, and ran off with Liam.

"I'm not silly," Tara said and began to cry. "Rose doesn't know. She can't!"

"Rose is not a baby," Paul said quietly. "She's much older than your baby was, so we never treat her as a baby, and when we explain things to her she understands and knows what is the truth. She believes in fairies and Santa Claus, but only as a kind of dream, and the idea of leprechauns is fun just as fairies are."

"Rose does believe in them so what will happen if they take her away?"

"If they tried, I think she'd object very strongly and scream," Paul said, laughing. "As they're only a kind of dream in the mind, they'd find her very heavy to carry. Even a baby would be hard to take away and what would they do with one if they did take him from a cot?"

Tara muttered something and Paul looked alarmed. "Who told you that, Tara? Answer me," he said firmly, and she looked up through her tears. "Tell me," he said more gently. "They can't hurt you, Tara."

"They will," she wailed. "I've said it and I shall be taken away to be punished."

"Who told you that? It was someone in the house, wasn't it?" She nodded and seemed unable to take her eyes off his stern but kind face. "Was it Mary?" Tara shook her head vigorously and Emma sensed Nuala's relief. "Was it one of your family?" She shook her head again, and Paul glanced at Nuala for help as he had no idea who else was in the household but the woman who had silently served them with breakfast.

Nuala mouthed the name "Myra", but shrugged as if that was impossible.

"It was Myra, wasn't it?"

Tara gave a muffled scream and clung to her mother, the two dolls falling unheeded to the ground.

Nuala gently put her away to sit on the log and said quietly, "Tell Paul, darling. We will all protect you."

Paul waited until the sobs subsided and Tara wiped away the tears with a handkerchief that Nuala handed to her. "What did she say?"

As if released, Tara said, "I asked Myra where the baby was, as he wasn't in the nursery and Mummy had told me not to go in there in case I caught something. Myra said the baby had been taken away." A shuddering sigh and a residual moan made way for a clearer voice. "Mummy came back from somewhere and was crying. I asked where Baby had gone and she said Baby was with Mary and Jesus, but after she'd left me alone, Myra came and said the leprechauns had taken Baby and would eat him for supper as they liked boy babies, but as I knew what had happened, I must never tell anyone or they'd come and get me and kill me and all the family. Myra laughed as if it was a joke, but I couldn't talk about it with Mummy or Daddy. Myra frightened me so much."

"The wickedness of it!" Nuala said.

"Listen to me," Paul said quietly. "Your baby had a nasty infectious disease called meningitis and had to be taken to hospital, where he died. Mummy came back very sad and thought you were too young to understand what had happened. She was so upset she couldn't talk about it, so she said what you heard in church, that the baby had gone to Jesus and Mary his mother, which means he had died."

"I didn't see him when he was dead." Tara sounded as if she didn't believe him. "I saw my grandad after *he* died, and we all had a party."

"He died of old age," Nuala said. "Baby couldn't be put in an open coffin for people to see and touch as he had a bad infectious disease. They had to bury him quickly."

"You have wakes for the dead?" Paul asked. "I often think we should do more like that. It shows everyone that the person really is dead and the family can say

121

goodbye but the dead person is still loved and life goes on."

"That's what I thought, until Baby died," Nuala said. "I blame myself for not talking about him to Tara. I was suffering too but as usual had to be strong for the rest of the family and thought Tara had got over it quickly even though she was quiet. Why didn't you tell me, Tara?" she asked bitterly.

"You were too close, and she was afraid for you and what would happen if she told anyone what Myra had said." Paul smiled. "That's what doctors like me are for, Nuala. People talk to us and we listen," he said simply.

"She'll have to go! I have had an evil woman cooking for us and being with my children."

"Is that necessary? I had the impression she's simple-minded, and maybe her head is full of old folklore. Has she ever hurt anyone except for this unfortunate happening?"

Nuala sighed. "We'll let Tara decide. It was very wicked of Myra to say those things to you and she must be told, but do you want her to leave?"

"No, Mummy. If she can say to me that she told lies, I want her to stay. She makes very nice barmbrack and washes my dolls' clothes." Tara was very calm now, she began to smile and looked at Paul with shining eyes. "Are you magic? I feel better."

"You're not just magic, you're an angel," Nuala said.

"Do you still want to hear my lecture on child psychology?" he said and laughed.

"More than ever. I want to know what I'm doing wrong!"

"Not a lot," Paul said softly. "You have a wonderful family and a bright future." He watched Tara walk away to see the other children. "Michael is an anthropologist and Tara is a very intelligent child. She could learn about local folklore from him, and be objective about it at an early age. It would stop her taking on half-baked ideas from people like Myra who almost believe what they say."

Nuala stood up and braced herself to see Myra. "She's a poor thing and we feel responsible for her as she has nobody of her own, but she must be told that if she ever frightens one of mine again she can go to the gypsies or Old Nick!"

"It's soup and sandwiches for lunch," Nuala said later. "I told Myra to stay away from me for the rest of the day and so I'm doing the cooking while she says her prayers, goes to confession and cries her eyes out! Sure it will do us all a power of good!"

"Let me help," Emma said.

"Can you make colcannon?"

"My Aunt Emily makes it and we often have it at home. She's half Irish and remembers what her mother taught her."

"We'll bring lamb chops back after the lecture and there's salad in the garden so we won't let them starve."

"Let me cut sandwiches," Emma said, and Nuala hugged her.

"It's like having a sister come home," she said. "It was a blessing from above when you and Paul came to Ireland."

"It's wonderful to be here," Emma said warmly. "You make us feel at home, and I know that Rose will hate to leave."

She buttered slices of bread and Nuala filled the sandwiches with ham and tomatoes, and put duck pâté and biscuits on a glass dish that looked as if it was a valuable antique. The Waterford glasses gleamed and made the simple cider and fruit juices look important.

"We must go to Waterford and buy glasses," Emma said. "It's time we had some decent glassware as we are entertaining more now."

"I'll come with you. I haven't been there for years." Nuala shrugged. "We had no need, as a lot of china and glass came to me with this house and Michael's family also left him many antiques and more glassware." She smiled. "We take it all for granted – nothing is made of the fact that we belong to very old Irish families." She sighed. "We still feel obligations to our tenants and people we employ, just as our ancestors did, which is why we put up with Myra. A lot of it goes back to the famine years when Ireland's potato crops failed and many starved or emigrated to escape it all. My family nearly starved with them as we gave what we had to our people and suffered with them, even if many believe that all the landowners turned their backs on the workers and their families."

"You still have land," Emma said.

"Only as far as the river on that side and the hill on the other; but it's enough, and we needed to sell a lot in my great-grandfather's time." She laughed. "We're well off by today's standards and we still have one racehorse which costs a fortune as he is stabled with the trainer."

"You must give me details, as Bea will be interested. You met her at Harvard, didn't you?"

"I met Dwight and Bea but not the children, as they were in Washington, but when we go over again I hope to visit them."

"Bea's father is thinking of buying a racehorse but it's a status symbol for him – he knows nothing about horses and would be scared to ride one."

"Why are you laughing, Mummy?" Liam held up grubby hands. "If I wash can I have something to eat? I'm starving."

"Lunch is ready," Nuala said and looked at the two flushed faces. "Aren't you a pair! Go and clean up and put on clean shirts. Do you need help, Rose?"

"I'll see to them," Emma said as Nuala put the food on the table. Tara walked in slowly. "I'm glad you know, Mummy. I was frightened you'd be taken away but I'm better now."

Nuala hugged her daughter and then asked what she wanted to drink, as if what had happened that morning was of no importance.

"Where's Myra?"

"I gave her time off," Nuala said shortly. "I sent her off to the priest for confession."

"Good. I hope he makes her say a hundred Hail Marys." Tara helped herself to a piece of cheese from the platter with more eagerness than she'd shown for weeks. "I'm hungry," she said, and Nuala saw the soft eyes and the smooth untroubled face that she'd thought were lost, and was glad to the point of tears.

Eleven

"I feel like celebrating," Nuala said. She smiled at Paul with real affection. "I loved your lecture and I shall never forget what you've done for Tara. Already she's the child I once knew and it's a miracle. I feel better myself, too, and know now that I should have seen what was happening to her and made sure she told me why she was withdrawn and frightened. I failed her because I was too involved with my own grief. Shall we have champagne tonight, Michael?"

"Anything you like, darling," Michael said. "Unless Paul has other ideas? We could eat out if that would help."

"What I'd really like, if it isn't a bore for you, is to go to a real Irish pub, drink Guinness and listen to a fiddle or two."

Emma recalled the intriguing sounds she had heard when she was too shy to go into the pub in Dublin. "Could we?" she asked eagerly.

"It's something we once did a lot but recently we just haven't seemed to get round to it, but it's a good idea. They serve food in Murphy's Barn and have good musicians, but there'll be no champagne, Nuala."

"A long cool glass of really good Guinness will do

nicely," Nuala said. She called for Mary and asked her if she would sit in for the children and give them supper, then suggested that Emma change into jeans and a light top and sweater. "They have a mixed bunch in Murphy's and we don't want to appear too dressed up. You'll like it," she added, as if Emma might be put off and expect a rough crowd in the bar.

"We couldn't do this if we were in a hotel with Rose," Paul pointed out as they changed for the evening. "You seem to be very much at home with Nuala, and Michael's a very interesting guy. I hope they visit us in London and stay for a while."

"Rose would like that – if Liam is invited too. It's strange but I feel as if Bea should be with us now, with her brood. They're so much alike. I hope we shall see more of this family in the future."

But when they sat on wooden chairs on the upper floor of the old pub to eat supper, looking down on the crowded bar and the group of musicians as if looking down from a minstrels' gallery, it was not Bea and her children who filled Emma's mind. A sensation of *déjà vu* that was completely unrealistic made her feel that Aunt Emily was just over there, out of sight, and Jane, her grandmother, was watching with the wry smile she had in her picture.

Emma sipped the smooth black stout and ate her seafood salad and soda bread while the musicians tuned up their fiddles and a few notes emerged from tin whistles and an old piano. A girl in a green skirt and white blouse sat on a stool and strummed gently on a washboard and as if they knew by instinct when to begin, the lively music came up to the gallery in perfect time and yet seeming to fit no time or pattern, but was almost hypnotic in its intensity and rhythm.

Paul looked at her and raised his glass. "To Emily and Janey," he said.

"And my grandmother," Emma whispered. "We came to the right place, Paul. I feel her here and the others are close."

"Sure it's the black stuff talking," he said in an exaggerated Irish accent.

"I love this place," Nuala said. "After a while I have enough of the fiddles but for an hour or so it's good and speaks of the past to me. It's very old and goes back beyond earlier troubles but thank God we are at peace here now and there is enough to eat in the villages. You said your grandmother was Irish, and tonight I see the touch of it in your face. You mentioned two aunts; they must have even more of the same look about them."

"They have dark hair and dark eyes and Aunt Emily is a bit fey."

"You're very lucky. That gift passed us by years ago; they said the gypsies stole it away." Nuala stopped. "I'm as bad as Myra! I must never say that in front of the children but it affects us all, Emma. We all have some regard for and slight fear of the little people. They were our fairy stories, told to us by sometimes ignorant servants and nannies whose whole lives were ruled by handed-down tales of what would happen if we displeased the little people. If we lose something, we say it was a gremlin who took it. It's handy to blame someone else for our own carelessness."

"With Aunt Emily and her family, it was the threat of being given to the gypsies that made them behave." Emma laughed. "It didn't work as they knew a family of Romanies who were highly respectable and my grandmother knew one woman very well, so that threat was no good. One uncle said he wanted to go with the gypsies, and he wore a red scarf at his throat as their boys did. He was a wild one."

Empty glasses were whisked away from the band and full glasses replaced them as they took a break and ate the food provided. The people in the gallery were in a cloud of cigarette smoke, loud laughter and incessant chatter, made gentle by the fumes of the cold black stout that was so easy to drink.

"This has been a wonderful experience," Paul said as they walked back to the house in the cool damp evening.

"I wish we could do more for you," Nuala said, almost tearfully. "Tara is a different girl, as if you released her from something evil."

"I did nothing," Paul insisted. "I was a strange but sympathetic face who asked the right questions. It's my job," he added flatly as he saw that Nuala was becoming maudlin.

"Some coffee, I think," Michael said and put an arm round his wife's shoulders. "Come along now, you never could drink enough to make a night of it. She didn't dance on the table but let's get some coffee into her," he added and laughed. "*In vino veritas*," he said softly. "We are for ever in your debt, Paul."

"No problems?" Nuala asked when a sleepy Mary opened the door to them.

129

"All asleep, but Liam had to be promised that he could take Rose to see the racehorse. I can do that with them on the bus, but you might like the outing too?"

"We'll all go tomorrow and you can visit your cousin. We'll drop you off in the village and you can take her some fruit."

"Not me, I'm afraid, as they want me tomorrow to see a couple of patients," Paul said. "I know," he added when he saw Emma's disapproval. "It isn't on my lecturing schedule and I didn't agree to see patients here but I'm interested, and I'm not exactly overworked."

"Men!" Nuala said. "Michael is taping songs in Gaelic and when he gets into the encampments, he's there all day." She laughed. "I tell him it isn't necessary to ask them to cook in the old ways just to please him, but he has eaten hedgehog baked in a mud coating and squirrel stewed in a pot with rabbit, potatoes and herbs, and vegetables that I probably pass every day of my life but would never pick to eat."

"You miss a lot." Michael poured more coffee. "Stick by me when we're stranded on a desert island. You might survive if you eat what I do."

"I'd want my coffee," Nuala replied.

"That's easy. During the war we had coffee made from dandelion roots and many people found a taste for it and still use it."

"I prefer a good recognisable brand of strong black coffee with no chicory added to make it go further." She yawned. "Dear God, I'm tired. See you tomorrow . . . or is it today?"

*   *   *

"It's blessedly quiet here after Dublin," Emma said at breakfast. "After all that music and the coffee late at night I thought I'd never sleep, but I went out like a light."

"A pure heart and a contented mind," Paul said.

"Is that your message for your patients today?"

"A contented mind, certainly, but the other is more difficult. I leave that to the priest to sort out if they are very wicked!"

"You are almost a confessor," Emma pointed out. "You often hear more about them than the priest will ever be told."

"I'm not with somebody for longer than the treatment and I'm not involved in their private lives, but a priest is always in the community and takes confession from families he sees every day. I have a feeling that not every small sin is confessed, though, and they tell more to a stranger. In a way it is like a confessional, as we do keep patient-doctor confidentiality."

"When I travelled on a slow train during the war, the carriage was often crammed with soldiers going on leave and it's amazing what they told me: things they said they'd not told to anyone but wanted to get off their chests. They knew they'd never see me again and it was a release." She shrugged. "I suppose I have a sympathetic face."

Paul laughed. "Did it really stop there?"

"What do you mean?"

"Did they never offer to carry your bags and suggest you met again? You have a very pretty face, not just a sympathetic one."

The dimples in her cheeks gave away her amusement under her regal stare. "That had nothing to do with it."

"But it happened?"

"It happened." She laughed. "It was impossible to know what they were really like. I saw the uniform and the worried expression, but who was to say if one man was more honest than another? I took the coward's way out and said I'd love to see them again but my boyfriend was meeting me and I couldn't let him down."

"I'm glad you were cautious, or who knows? We wouldn't have met and you might be married to someone you found you didn't like."

"A ward full of lusty men with broken limbs, otherwise good health but lots of testosterone floating about soon taught me caution! In bed, in hospital pyjamas, they often showed very little outward sign of what they did and who they were in civvy life and I had a few shocks when I saw men who came to say goodbye on the day they were discharged as fit. They dressed in their own clothes, somehow taking on a personality with which they were more comfortable. Sometimes it was horrific. I never did like oxblood suits and winklepicker shoes. Often the quiet ones dressed well, and I could imagine them holding down responsible jobs before they were called up. A hospital ward is a great leveller, though, and most of them got along well together."

"Must go." Paul kissed her and picked up his briefcase. "Nuala said she'll take you in the Land Rover, so I can use the car. I should be back by dinnertime."

"Don't promise to see more cases than you want to

do," Emma warned. "Even *you* can't sort out the minds of the whole nation!"

"Patrick Hanratty wants me to hold his hand while he uses Thiopentone on two men who have shown little sign of recovery under conventional physiotherapy and tranquilliser drugs. Not many doctors here use hypnosis, and in cases of battle fatigue it's sometimes necessary to unlock the causes of things like functional paralysis. Patients often labelled malingerers are really ill. If I'd seen my best friend killed by a sniper and was knee-capped in a revenge attack, I think my mind would refuse to let me function properly even after the wounds healed, so I might convince myself that I was unable to walk just to avoid more conflict."

"You're getting enthusiastic," she warned him. "Have a good day, but make no other promises – we leave for Belfast next week, and you have more lectures to give."

"Everything is under control! I worry more about you. We have no room in Kensington for a thoroughbred racehorse and, dare I say it, we can't afford one."

Rose wanted to wear trousers as they were going to the stables. "It isn't like the one in America," Emma told her. "We're going to see horses in clean, neat racing stables and we'll have lunch in the country."

Nuala laughed. "Rose can wear a pair of jeans that no longer fit Liam. I can't imagine them coming back here without dirtying their clothes, so we might as well expect the worst."

"What is your horse called?"

"Tyrone of Ballykelly."

Rose wrinkled her nose. "When I have a horse I shall call him Max."

"Just Max?" asked Nuala. "That wouldn't look very impressive in the stud book."

"Max is a good name. He'd come if I called him that."

"We call ours Ty for short," Nuala admitted. "Are you coming with us, Tara?"

"I'm all ready, Ma, but Patrick is staying to meet Dermot from the farm. He said he'll wear a hard hat if he rides, so don't worry."

Nuala put extra sweaters in the Land Rover. "I remember being frozen the last time we went there as the wind sometimes sweeps over the hill. We'll take anoraks too and a change of clothes for the children: the restaurant is more formal than most and won't welcome children smelling of horses. We shall be warm once we go in for lunch."

The racing stables were quiet, and Nuala was told that the horses were out on the hill being exercised but were due back soon. Another family sat waiting for the string to return and Liam called out to the boy: "Play five stones?"

"No, you beat me the last time," protested the other child. He took a ball from his pocket and Liam wandered off with him to throw it against a stable wall.

"That boy's American," Rose said. "I wonder if he knows Mark?"

"America is a very big place," Emma reminded her. "We don't know everyone in London, and America is much bigger."

Rose went closer to the two boys but stood back when they started wrestling. Liam was laughing so Nuala shrugged and let them play.

"I hate rough boys," Rose said. "I don't want to play with them. That boy is spotty."

"Sam!" His father called him over and told him not to play with the other children. He smiled at Emma almost guiltily and sent a very sulky boy to sit in the car.

"I thought the boys were playing well for once," Nuala said. "That couple were quite friendly when we met them at the races, but maybe they think Liam is too rough."

"Sam has spots," Rose said again and Emma was alarmed.

"How many? Just a few on his face?"

"Lots and lots," Rose said with satisfaction.

Nuala walked over to the American couple and smiled. "Is something wrong?" she asked.

Sam's father looked very embarrassed. "We thought it would be fine out here in the fresh air with nobody about, then you turned up and Sam wanted to play. It was OK until they started on a tussle so I don't know what to say."

"Just tell me what the spots are," Nuala said sweetly, but her expression told him she needed a truthful answer.

"It's what all children have and it's nothing," he said defensively, then lowered his voice and said, "It's chickenpox."

"Praise be for that. It would be different if it was German measles."

"What's the difference?"

"My guest has to go back to England into a house where there's a pregnant girl."

He looked puzzled, and his wife stared at Nuala and lit a cigarette.

"You do know that if a pregnant woman is exposed to German measles, she might have a deformed baby?" Nuala said bluntly. "Are you sure it's only chickenpox?"

"Yes, we took him to the doctor and he told us," Sam's mother said.

"It could be worse," Nuala said with an air of resignation. "We'll look for spots in a week or so, after they were in such close contact just now."

"Sam isn't feeling ill and he has fewer spots today."

Nuala took Liam into the clubhouse and made him take off his jacket and change his jeans. "Maybe all the germs are on his clothes," she said hopefully and wrapped his top clothes in a towel, separate from the other things in the boot of the Land Rover.

The horses circled the yard, ridden by slender lads who had the same easy, almost casual manner as the ones they'd seen in the gypsy camp. "They all have the same ambition," Nuala said. "They want to ride a winner in a big race; and this is the best way to get on the books as a jockey after an apprenticeship here."

Rose stayed close to her mother, and even Liam seemed daunted by the tall sleek animals who bore no similarity to the sturdy ponies and donkeys he had ridden. "That's ours," he said at last and a stable boy nodded.

"The one with the white flash is it? He's a fine ride."

"I want to be a jockey." Liam looked at the lad with admiration.

"Don't get too big, or the horses won't take you,"

136

he was told. "How will you like mucking out for many months before you ever get to ride one of these?" He winked at Nuala.

Liam turned down his mouth. "I hate doing that," he said.

Nuala laughed. "Another career abandoned before it started. 'We've thought of being a train driver, a fireman and now a jockey, but Liam doesn't like hard work or getting up early." She rumpled his hair. "But he does like eating. Now what's it to be, Liam?"

In the restaurant they were served with watercress soup and roast duck, but Liam asked for bacon and scrambled eggs and Rose copied him. "He's a pain," Nuala said. "We bring him out for a treat and he has what he can have any day at home. This is delicious. Myra has no hand for duck. She overcooks it no matter how often I tell her to leave it pink in the middle, so we hardly ever eat it at home unless I cook it."

They watched a horse being exercised in the pool and when Nuala persuaded Liam that it was a pool for horses and not for little boys he lost interest. "Where's Sam?" he asked.

Emma told him she'd seen a car driven away by Sam's father, who had said they would stop off at a pub and eat out of doors away from people and go back to their rented apartment. "Kids!" he'd said. "This was supposed to be a holiday to take in a race or two, check on our horse and see Ireland, but Sam has ruined it. We feel like lepers and he gets tetchy in the evenings. I hope Liam doesn't pick it up," he added.

Twelve

"I'll have to go soon," Paul said. "I've stayed much longer here than I'd planned, but some of the work is relevant to Belfast as well as Dublin, and we've been in contact on the telephone. Connor was due to lecture in Belfast after me but he's changed round and that's given me a bit more time here."

"I shall be sorry to leave," Emma admitted. "Fortunately Nuala seems to want us to stay as long as we can, and the children get on very well, but we have been here for at least a week longer than anticipated, so Belfast, here we come."

"I'll ring about accommodation tomorrow," Paul said. "They offered me rooms in the university but I doubt if it would be private enough for three of us there, and it could be noisy."

"Nuala made me promise to come back for a few days on our way home, so we could leave some luggage here and pick it up on our return."

"You can pack later. Let's walk over to the paddock and say hello and goodbye to Sligo and Kavanagh." Paul grinned. "It's a pity we can't take a donkey home with us but we have no stable and I think Mrs Coster would object to dirty hooves on her nice hall floor!"

Emma raised an eyebrow. "A house-trained donkey? I don't believe there is such an animal."

"Rose? Liam? Anyone coming for a walk?"

Liam sidled into the room. "I'm not feeling well."

"We're going to see Kavanagh."

"Go on then," he said sulkily.

Emma bent down and looked at him more closely. The day before he'd been tired and wanted lots of cool drinks, yet had eaten well and played snap with Rose, but now he did look unwell. "Have you a pain?" she asked. He shook his head and rubbed his eyes. Emma unbuttoned the collar of his shirt and knew what to expect before she saw the spots. It was about right for the incubation period – there was no doubt that Liam had chickenpox.

"No walk now," she said to Paul. "I'd better see if Rose is all right."

Rose was asleep on the huge settee and Emma looked down at her flushed cheeks. "I don't think we can go to Belfast."

"Rose too?"

"A couple of spots on her face, which means there are many more on her body, and I think a raised temperature. I thought both the children were off colour a few days ago but hoped it was just because they were dashing about so much."

"Those Americans are not the most popular people I've met over here," Paul said grimly. "What are we to do? I shall have to go to Belfast alone, which is no problem, but we have a sick child who can't travel home on crowded ferries."

"And I must stay with her," Emma said.

"I hear you've seen Liam?" Nuala asked cheerfully. "He's very proud of his spots and says that Rose has them too, all over her back and tummy." She laughed. "A bit early to play doctors and nurses, but once again they have something in common . . . chickenpox."

"I can't take Rose to Belfast," Emma began, but Nuala shrugged aside her problem.

"I've asked Mary to make up the two small beds in the big room overlooking the garden. It will give us more space to look after them and they can compare spots to their hearts' content."

"I don't know what to say."

"The less said the better. It was our fault for letting Liam play with Sam, and this is easier if they have each other's company. Tara and Patrick had it when they were quite small so Tara can read to them if they feel a bit limp. I'll see what I have in the medicine chest. There should be some calamine lotion if it isn't all dried up, and we can get that easily from the local chemist."

"Do we have to call the doctor?"

"I'll ask him to look in. He enjoys a sherry before lunch so he'll be here about twelve if his past routine is anything to go by."

Mary put the two children to bed and gave them drinks. For once, neither of them wanted to play, soon drifting off to sleep. Emma packed a bag for Paul and decided rather guiltily that she would rather be with Rose and Nuala's family than kicking her heels in Belfast while she waited for Paul to finish lectures.

She glanced at the local newspaper and saw that another bomb had been set off in the Shankhill Road in Northern Ireland. She prayed that Paul would be safe.

"If I stay on the university campus I shall be away from any violence," he reassured her later. "These incidents make it even more essential for me to talk about stress and battle fatigue: some people still believe that there is no such malady, so people suffering are getting no help. Their attitude is as bad as that in the First World War, when men were hounded and sometimes shot for malingering."

"Be very careful," Emma said with vehemence. "Come back soon as we shall miss you. This is the first time we've been separated in a strange country and I hate it."

"The separation or the country?" he asked lightly.

She kissed his cheek. "The separation of course. I still love Ireland."

"Why do I feel a sense of relief that you aren't coming to Belfast? I suppose, in the back of my mind, I worry we could be taking Rose into danger. I shall give my lectures and maybe take a few sessions and come back as soon as I can, then we must go home."

"The spots are out" – Emma returned to the subject of Rose – "which means that they were infectious for a few days before that, so who knows how many local people they've infected?"

"Nuala hasn't had small children in the house lately, and we kept Liam and Rose out of the village because people who Nuala knows insisted on giving them too many sweets, so I can't think they've spread their

141

little gift to anyone. I'm a bit rusty on infectious diseases. How long is the quarantine period after the spots are out?"

"A week after the spots have turned to little blisters and dried out," Emma said. "Most of the infection is spread before the spots appear but after that they recover fast. At least they don't have more serious symptoms like pain in the legs and muscles and very high temperatures."

Emma helped Mary give the children cool sponge baths and anointed them with calamine lotion until they looked like clowns in pinky-white make-up, which caused a lot of amusement. "You look like two ghosts," Tara said. "Ghosts with little red spots in the white make-up."

The doctor came and went, spending more time over his two large glasses of sherry than with the children. Nuala was relieved. "It's nothing, nothing at all," she asserted firmly.

"He hardly looked at them!"

"Don't underestimate him, Emma. He's a marvellous doctor if something is really bad, but he took one look at those two and said it was a mild infection. With you here, he was confident that we were doing all the right things and he might pop in to see them in a few days' time . . . when it will all be over and the sherry decanter will be topped up," Nuala added, with a laugh.

Paul telephoned every night and sounded bored with life in student accommodation, although he had dinner each evening with the professors in their more sumptuous dining room.

"Is it a busy hospital?" Emma asked when he told her he'd treated two patients who were recovering from bullet wounds but showed no signs of taking an interest in life.

"One advantage of a busy hospital is that they want to discharge patients as quickly as possible to make way for more urgent cases, so the ones I'm seeing will go to a convalescent hospital outside Belfast, with lovely views of the mountains. There's growing concern about the psychological harm done by violence and I hope I'm making sure that more doctors see what can be done by analysis under hypnosis."

"Surely the convalescent home is the place to do such work, in peaceful surroundings."

"I hope to go there for two days and do just that, starting tomorrow," Paul said. "I'm trying to collect a team to carry on after I leave, and there've been all the right murmurings, so after my visit to the Mountains of Mourne I shall be back with you and Rose."

"Buy some cards of local views. I envy you that visit: I wanted to go there, but I know it's impossible as according to Rose we have a very sick child. She tells me that when she wants something! I think she could have a career as an actress. I am a bit bored: all I do is stay here, dab on pink lotion and read the same books endlessly when Tara says she's had enough."

"Not long now, darling. I'm bored too. Suddenly, I want to see the London streets and have Mick tell me off for spending too much time with certain patients."

"We can go home at any time now. The vesicles have almost dried up and Rose and Liam are playing normally, but we still keep them in one room," Emma said. "I'll go into Dublin for last-minute shopping and be ready whenever you say we can leave."

With Mary in charge of the children, Nuala said she'd take Emma out to lunch in Dublin. "We deserve it, and the children are almost well, so let's make the most of this spell of fine weather and forget calamine lotion and Beatrix Potter books for a couple of hours."

"I feel almost civilised," Emma said as she pushed aside her depleted lobster and drank the last of her glass of white wine.

"I'm sorry you have to go back," Nuala said. "It's as if I'd found a long-lost sister."

"I feel the same. I wish we lived closer to each other. Rose will miss Liam, too, and I don't think Jean will fill that gap. However, I've bought toys for both of them and that will make their next meeting easy. It's a pity Clive's left, as Rose adores him, but Margaret wanted to get the apartment in Hampshire ready for the baby and for George to have a good welcome home when the Navy sends him back. She sounded very excited when I got through eventually on the phone last night and I think she's very happy and healthy."

"She's lucky to be pregnant," Nuala said wistfully. "I wanted more children, but after the last one I was advised to forget that and concentrate on the family I have."

"You have three healthy children." Emma tried to

sound objective. "I have one and hope for more but as yet we haven't been lucky."

Nuala smiled. "And what has that fey aunt of yours to say about that? I envy you such a relative. I can imagine her sitting with her feet on the fender round the fire, drinking strong tea laced with whiskey and sharing her gift of second sight."

"She doesn't do that all the time. She's a very shrewd woman and half of what she tells people is plain common sense." Emma laughed. "She has never been to Ireland and has no desire to do so but she was excited when I said we were coming here, as if the visit would be good for me in many ways."

"It has been for me," Nuala said. "Michael and I will never forget that in half an hour Paul released Tara from fear and made her glow again. You may shake your head and smile but it's true. One thing is true of the Irish, we never forget a good deed done to us and never forget a bad one." She sighed. "That may account for the troubles here."

"Back to Beatrix Potter, unless there's something more interesting in that bookshop."

"Too young, too old, and I'm not reading that one out loud or I'll weep," Nuala said dismissively as they looked through the stock.

"And this one would bring leprechauns back into the conversation again, so not that one," Emma added. They bought picture books of horses and farm animals and *The Wind in the Willows* for reading aloud and went home refreshed.

Rose was playing with Plasticine and showed Emma

a deformed animal, bright green with one leg shorter than the others as she had run out of green. "It's Sligo," she explained. "Can we go and see the donkeys?"

"I don't see why not. You could do with some fresh air, and a short walk will be fine, but no riding today as you both have a few drying spots."

"We'll take them some carrots," Liam said. "We won't ride them and we won't give them spots."

"A spotty donkey would be very strange," Emma replied, and dressed the two children warmly as there was a chill in the air that hinted at the coming autumn.

A few yellow leaves fluttered slowly down as they reached the paddock and Emma felt a pang of loss at the thought of autumn, the end of growth and the release of summer leaves. Who knew what might be in store? She remembered crunching dry leaves underfoot as she walked from the villa where the nurses lived to the main hospital when she was nursing wounded soldiers in Surrey. Autumn had always been a poignant time for her. It was in autumn that she'd braved the home on the Downs in Bristol and begun her nursing career, which turned her entire world upside-down.

She shook off the sudden depression, convinced that she was merely sad at the thought of leaving Nuala and the warm, intimate life of the family in Ireland. She held out a carrot to Kavanagh.

Rose watched her face and said, "Why are you sad, Mummy?"

"Not really sad, but we'll be sorry to leave Liam and the others when Daddy finishes teaching in Belfast."

"I don't want you to go!" Liam shouted and Sligo bucked away from the noise.

"You'll be coming to London to see us, and we can go to some lovely places," Emma said hastily.

"Promise?"

"Your mummy will come too and we'll all have a great time."

"You can get chocolate from a machine on the boat and write your name," Rose said, "and when we get home you can see the Changing of the Guard just like Christopher Robin did, and feed the ducks."

"Goodbye, donkeys," Emma said. "You've had all the carrots and now it's time for our elevenses."

"There's been a call from Paul," Nuala said when they got indoors. "It's nothing to worry you but he wanted you to hear it from him and not from the news."

"Is he all right?"

"Sure and he's fine, but a bomb dropped close to the university and destroyed a few walls. Paul's now on his way to the other hospital where, please God, they will not hurt him or the poor men already damaged," Nuala said fervently.

"Did he say when he'd be back here?"

"The day after tomorrow. We'll have a farewell dinner at Murphy's Barn and shed a few tears at your leaving us."

"I'd better pack a few things. It's amazing what I've bought since we came here."

"A few sweeteners for your staff," Nuala said shrewdly. "Do they expect so much?"

147

"I know I may have overdone that part, but Eileen and Mick are very precious, both as employees and as friends, and I hope that when we're home again the girls will find what they once had in common. After all, they will share memories of Ireland," she added hopefully.

"Don't push it. They're obviously different in many ways and you must accept it. Rose likes the boys best and I think Jean might be happier with girls and dolls."

"You're right, and when they go to school they will both make other friends."

Emma glanced at her watch for the third time. "You can't wait to set eyes on him, can you?" Nuala said and laughed.

Emma blushed. "It's ridiculous to feel like this after being married for so long, but the bomb scare made me want to gather him up and make sure he was safe."

"You can do that tonight," Nuala said mischievously. "Not now! I hear the car, so we can eat before I starve. Paul said he'd be here by lunchtime and he just made it."

"I smell Irish stew," Paul said after he'd kissed Emma.

"And I smell chocolate," Rose said hopefully.

"After lunch when I unpack my bag," Paul promised, and hugged her. "No spots?" he asked.

"All gone, and we're clear to go home according to the doctor."

"You just missed him, but he did leave enough sherry for us to have a glass before lunch," Nuala said.

"We do have spots," Liam said firmly. "Lots and lots and you can't go home."

"You will see us again soon," Emma said.

"You can't go! I'll never come to your house, and you'll forget all about me."

Paul took him by the hand. "There's a big calendar in Daddy's study. Let's make a mark on it to show when you will be coming to London. That mark will make it certain and you can see how quickly the time goes before you do come to us."

He glanced at Nuala, who nodded and suggested a date in about a month's time. Liam went off happily with Paul to ruin his father's neat calendar with crayon smudges.

"Can you manage that date?" asked Emma.

"My time is flexible, and Mary can cope while we're away. I doubt if Patrick would want to leave just now as he's helping to gentle a foal and thinks he's the world's best trainer." She sighed. "The summer goes too fast. I was forgetting that they'll both be at school and not have time to come to England, but Liam and I can come."

Paul telephoned Mick to make sure that a car would be ready to pick them up from the ferry port for the long drive home, and suddenly London seemed very near. "We can leave this hire car at the ferry terminal so our luggage will be easy to manage there; we'll take our time to drive back from Wales to London." He grinned. "Time enough for us to get used to the idea of going back to work."

Dinner in Murphy's Barn was as good as the first time and the fiddles and tin whistles were in great form, but

149

the party in the gallery didn't stay late and went back to the house in a sober frame of mind.

"Don't be sad," Paul said when they were ready for bed. "Ireland isn't far away and you have a real bond now. Nuala will be in London before you know it and even Rose is looking forward to showing off to Jean."

"I know, but I shall miss Nuala very much. It's almost like being with Bea, but different."

"That's a bit Irish!"

"You know what I mean."

"Come to bed. Our last night in Ireland and our last night with nothing on our minds but each other and the way we are in love."

"It's wonderful to have you back," Emma whispered. "I was frightened when I heard of the bomb and wanted to hold you close to protect you."

"You can do that now," he said.

Thirteen

"I contacted Mick and explained that we're staying the night at a hotel halfway between the ferry and home as Rose is still a little fragile and weepy after leaving Liam and Tara, and the journey seems to be worrying her more than usual."

"Everything under control at home?" Emma asked.

Paul laughed. "It's just as well Rose had chickenpox in Ireland, as there's an epidemic in London and the Home Counties and Jean came out in spots yesterday."

"That's a relief. I thought we were safe to go home, but there was a niggling doubt about Rose being able to pass it on even though the doctor said she was well over the infection. I would hate Jean to have caught it from Rose."

"I bet she doesn't have as many spots as we did," Rose said.

"I should keep quiet about that. She may have lots more than you," Paul replied. He eyed her quizzically. "Don't you like Jean any more?"

"I do like her, but she can get anything she wants if she cries and you don't let me have as much as that." Rose went red. "I do like her but I hate her when she cries for things and tries to take mine."

"Does she do that?" Emma was worried.

"She tries, but I stop her and then we quarrel."

"Are the things that Jean cries for what you want?" Paul asked.

"No, they're silly things like dolls' clothes which I don't really want," Rose admitted.

"I don't see that you have a problem," Paul said. "You have lots of things that Jean doesn't have and you don't care for dolls."

Rose laughed. "It's fun making her cross, Daddy. She didn't like me playing with Clive or talking about Mark, and her friends aren't nice so she tries to take my things."

Paul looked serious. "Remember this, Rose. Jean didn't go to America and you did, Jean didn't have Mark and the other two children to play with and you did, Jean didn't have a lot of treats that you had when Clive and his mummy were here, and Jean doesn't have Aunt Emily and you have. She feels left out, so you must be nice to her. You are the lucky one." He ruffled her hair. "Maybe if we left you to stay with Mick and Eileen and Jean you could ask for whatever you wanted."

"No, Daddy. I want to stay with you. You wouldn't give me to them, would you?" she asked anxiously.

He hugged her tightly. "Never. We love our naughty, nice little girl and we want to keep her, but you must learn to share more with Jean. If she tries to be silly, just walk away and do something else."

"I can tell her nicely about Ireland and the donkeys. She doesn't like donkeys so she won't want one," Rose said, as if making a concession. She looked up slyly.

"What have you bought for us when we get home? I felt two parcels but couldn't see inside and I know they are for us."

"Miss Fiddle Fingers must wait," Paul said. "I might have bought some things, but they might be for Christmas," he teased.

Rose flung her arms round him. "Now I *know* they're for us."

"At least she seems to want to go home now," Emma said. "I do too. Having got this far away from Ireland, I look forward to seeing old friends and we shall see Nuala and Liam again very soon."

"You may have to take over from Eileen for a while if Jean is very demanding," Paul pointed out.

"Good. I shall enjoy that, but I shall never take over her place in the household again. I can relieve her for breaks, and Rose need not be isolated from Jean as it's unlikely that she'll be infected again."

Kensington was quiet and the leaves on the trees lining the streets sighed softly as if nothing was urgent. The two bay trees guarding the entrance to the house and clinic were freshly trimmed into elegant round shapes on slender trunks, and it was evident that Mrs Coster had given the steps an extra special welcoming scrub.

"Dwight and Bea made sure we would never forget them," Paul said when he saw the bay trees. "Remember the day when Dwight staggered in with those trees? They were terribly expensive but he insisted they added a lot of tone to the house, to impress private patients, and so they have."

"I think of Bea each time I come through that doorway," Emma agreed, and hurried into the hall.

Rose ran up the stairs into her bedroom and put her small case on the bed. "Can I see Jean now, Mummy?"

"Not yet. I'll go down to their flat and see if Eileen is there and ask her if Jean is ready for visitors. I don't think Eileen is in the kitchen." Emma walked slowly down the side staircase. The kitchen was not as tidy as usual and there was dirty washing-up left on the draining board. Of course, she told herself. Robert was now living in the house and he might have had a meal at an odd time between cases. If Eileen was busy with Jean she would leave such minor details until she was free.

"Oh, sister! You're back!" Eileen burst into tears.

Emma was alarmed. "What's wrong? How is Jean?"

"She's so difficult, and I've never had to nurse a very sick child in my whole life," Eileen said, dramatically.

"She's very ill?"

"The doctor says not, and hints that she's shamming, but they aren't always right. Jean says she feels ill and wants me here all the time. I can't get on with my work until she drops off to sleep. Last night I was up until midnight polishing the sitting room ready for you today."

"If you aren't used to illness it is very confusing," Emma agreed tactfully. "Is she really feeling ill or is she enjoying the time you give to her?"

"She wouldn't put it on," Eileen said, in a shocked voice.

"Oh yes she would," Mick said from the doorway. "Eileen spoils her something rotten and then wonders why Jean plays up."

"That's not true, Mick Grade." Eileen was close to tears again, so Mick shrugged and went back up to the office to brief Paul on what had been happening while he was away.

"Let me see her," Emma said. She opened the bedroom door and stood by the bed, smiling at Jean, who was sitting up surrounded by toys. "Hello, spotty," she said cheerfully.

Jean looked annoyed as she detected the lack of awe that a sick child should generate.

"I'm very ill," she muttered.

"Then all you'll want to do is sleep and have drinks," Emma said kindly. "I'll tell Rose that you're too sick to have visitors. If you sleep now, your mummy can get on with her work; you'll soon be better and then you can play."

"I want . . ." began Jean, then stopped before her mother could rush to her side, as Emma was in the way.

"You seem to have everything there," Emma said firmly. "Toys and books and a drink on the table, and you can take yourself to the lavatory."

"I want to see Rose," she whined in a plaintive little-girl voice.

"When you're better and not needing to have your mother with you all the time," Emma said firmly. "We all have work to do and I need Mummy upstairs, so be quick and ask for anything you *really* need now, and she will bring you your supper after you've had a nap."

Jean gave her an angry look and sank into the bedclothes with the sheet over her head.

"She's upset," Eileen said accusingly.

"Yes, I think she is," Emma said in a clear voice that penetrated the bedclothes. "She'll be fine alone until suppertime. I'll explain to Rose that she can't see Jean until she's better and not making such a fuss over a few spots. She'll be disappointed, as she wants to show what we bought in Ireland, but she'll have to wait." She paused as if turning to Eileen, speaking in a lower voice. "It's not much fun for Rose if Jean whines all the time and doesn't play nicely, so I'll keep her upstairs until Jean's feeling brighter. Come along, Eileen, I want to hear all about what's been happening while we were away, and we must arrange a rota of work that I can share with you until Jean is up and about." She shepherded the reluctant Eileen out of the room and closed the door behind her.

"What if she needs something?"

"She doesn't need anything but a good rest," Emma said firmly; and when Eileen crept down half an hour later, Jean was fast asleep and soon Eileen was laughing with Emma about the many good moments they had enjoyed in Ireland.

"Mick loved the stout," Eileen said. "We met some nice people and I liked the music in the pubs. Mick won fifty pounds at the races and he's put that aside towards our next holiday, whenever that may be. We might be able to go to a really nice hotel."

"We started out in a good hotel but we were very bored. I was so glad to go to a private house and have the company of the family there. Rose made friends with Liam, the smallest child of the family, and they rode donkeys and did a lot of things they couldn't do in a hotel."

"Jean doesn't like boys," Eileen said. "Clive teased her and said that dolls were silly."

"Clive is old enough to know better. I'm sure he didn't mean to be unkind."

"What really upset her was that you took him and Rose to see the Changing of the Guard without her."

"Has she ever said she wanted to go there?"

"Well, no," Eileen admitted. "Mick tried to take her once but she began to cry and said she didn't want to see big rough men marching." Eileen looked thoughtful. She put away a couple of casserole dishes and dried some plates. "Mick says Jean is getting to be a pain in the neck and must come to terms with the fact that she can't have everything. But when I was little I had nothing much, and so I suppose I do spoil her."

"That's understandable, but if you spoil a child, the real treats mean nothing," Emma pointed out. "Obviously you want the best for Jean, but she will value occasional gifts more than if she asks for something and has it straight away."

"She keeps on about a leppercorn," Eileen said. "She said that Rose is bringing one home and she gets upset when she thinks she isn't going to have one."

Emma laughed. "We had a problem there. Rose was convinced that leprechauns were real and could grant her wishes, but we have managed to show her that they are just imaginary, like fairies, and that the dolls they make dressed in green are just toys."

"Jean did want one." Eileen sounded almost frightened of what the child would say or do if thwarted, and Emma made a mental note to hold the dolls in reserve until Jean's outlook was less anti-social.

Emma cooked dinner for Robert, Paul, Rose and herself; Mick and Eileen went down to their own apartment. Rose nodded with sleepiness and went to bed without fuss while the adults sat talking over glasses of wine.

"Joan's working this evening," Robert said.

"I'm looking forward to seeing her again," Emma assured him. "She's made the spare room very comfortable, and the sooner you get married the sooner you can move in together, except when you want to stay in Covent Garden."

"We want to have a very private ceremony, with only about a dozen guests including you and Paul. Joan doesn't want a white wedding in church, so I thought a civil ceremony sometime next month might be suitable."

"That's wonderful. If it's such a small party, we can have the reception here. It will be fun," Emma stated firmly when she saw his doubtful expression.

"What time off do you want?" Paul asked. "Take what you need: the clinic's running smoothly and we can cut down on appointments for non-urgent cases for a week or so."

"We thought we could go to Cornwall for a week, but we both want to come back after that and settle down to living together. Joan can take leave and come back to work in casualty on a part-time basis."

"Gradually the house is filling up, but we still have

room for guests," Paul said. "You'll like Nuala and her small dynamo, Liam."

"Will all this be too much for Eileen? She has her hands full with Jean and seems unsettled."

"She will be fine. As the spots disappear and Jean gets bored with being an invalid, Eileen can get back to work and leave Jean to play alone, or with Rose when I allow it."

Robert looked impressed. "You've managed to keep Rose away from the flat?" He grinned. "A brilliant psychological move, Emma. I can't imagine Jean staying in bed now, if she thinks she may be missing something."

Paul frowned. "It's difficult to undo the damage to a spoiled child, but we can't risk Rose becoming like her. I think she realised that we wouldn't let her be as bad as Jean when we were in Ireland. A healthy, selfish boy did wonders for her and she is very reasonable now."

"I feel sorry for Mick and Eileen," Emma said. "Tomorrow, I shall send them off to the pictures together after they've given Jean her supper, and I'll keep an eye on her." She stood up and sighed. "I'm sleepy, but I must unpack more of the clothes or they'll be a mass of creases."

"We'll do the washing-up," Robert promised. "That is if we have the energy after that lovely meal."

The cases, open on the bed, looked formidable but Emma sorted out clothes for washing and pressing and hung the rest away. She brought a black suit out of the closet and wondered if it needed dry-cleaning. It was a suit she'd bought at the height of the popularity of clothes worn by Jacqueline Kennedy. Every other girl with a reasonable figure had worn the smartly cut jackets and pencil-slim skirts topped by the Jacqui pillbox hat, and Emma had discarded the outfit as she hated to be one of a crowd; but now, with other accessories, it might be useful.

She slipped out of her dress and pulled the skirt on, then found the zip was difficult to do up and the waist button was impossible. "Damn!" she said softly.

The food in Ireland and the additional leisure had not been exactly slimming, but she had no idea she'd added so much to her waistline. She thought back. The suit had been close-fitting and she had always changed out of it as soon as she came home from meeting friends as the waistband was tight, but this was more than that. Slowly she put it back on the hanger and found that her heart was beating fast.

She opened her handbag and took out her diary. The visit to Ireland was clearly marked and so were the usual circles indicating her periods. She had been so busy and involved with other matters that she'd forgotten to check – she hadn't had a period for over two months!

Emma sat on the bed, not knowing if she wanted to laugh or cry. She ran her fingers over her breasts and found them slightly fuller than usual. Her face in the mirror seemed the same, but pale, and her excitement grew, then faded. It must be a false alarm. She had no morning sickness and felt fine.

"Finished?" Paul asked and looked up from his book. "What's wrong?" He put the book down and stood up. "You look pale. Was the journey so bad? We've been selfish. I should have taken you out for a meal instead of you having to cook for all of us."

"It isn't that." She buried her face in his jacket and he had to bend over her to hear the words. "I think I'm pregnant, Paul." She raised her face to his and he was almost overwhelmed by her sudden serene beauty and his own elation. "Tell me it's true," she whispered. "I'm a month overdue but I've had no sickness, so is it a false alarm? If it is I don't think I can bear it."

"Do you feel as you did when you were expecting Rose?"

"No, I feel wonderful."

"We can't diagnose you tonight as obstetrics is not my subject, but I'll ring Stella in the morning and you can see her as soon as possible. She will tell you the truth and not make half-baked assumptions." He laughed. "Unless you want to consult Mrs Coster first? She has all the experience in the world after her brood and must have known people with pregnancies without sickness."

"I'll stick to Stella," Emma said firmly, but her colour returned and she smiled normally. "I mustn't think of it yet, but this convinces me how much I want another baby."

"We'll keep this to ourselves until we know if it's certain," Paul said. "Just make sure you lift no heavy weights or strain yourself in any way."

He made her sit down in an armchair and brought her hot milk with chocolate powder in it, her favourite treat when she was tired or overworked.

"Biscuit? I found some in a tin that Bea left here and they seem to be OK. What's the matter? Too hot?"

A seraphic smile as she thrust the hot drink away was full of triumph. "That tastes horrible," she said. "I fancy some Bovril."

"We're not going through that again, are we?" he asked in mock despair.

"It was tea the last time," she said complacently. "I really do think I *am*!"

The phone rang and Paul answered it. "We were going to ring you tomorrow but it's lovely to hear from you," he said warmly. "Here she is."

"Aunt Emily?"

"Who else? You sound in good form." Emily giggled. "How are you? Was it very good in Ireland? I had your card and it's time you came down here for a few days to be fed and rested. Rose too, after her chickenpox."

"I may do that, but Jean has chickenpox now and Eileen isn't very good at dealing with her as she's very spoiled and demanding."

"All the more reason for you to come away. You don't want to do much just now. Think of yourself for once and let them sort out their own affairs."

"It was Rose who had chickenpox, not me! I'm fine."

"Good. I'll expect you next week, and I expect Margaret will come over for a day to see you." She chuckled. "You have things in common."

"Aunt Emily! How can you possibly know? I only found out this evening and I haven't been seen by Stella yet!"

"I saw it before you went to Ireland. I knew it would happen there and I was right, wasn't I?"

"Yes," Emma said softly. "I'm glad it started there."

"Does Rose know?"

"Not yet. I have to get used to the idea first and choose the time carefully – after I've seen Stella to confirm it."

"It's different this time."

"What do you mean?"

"You sound very well and you aren't being sick," Emily said.

"Is that all you can tell me?" Emma tried to hide her disappointment.

"Margaret asked me if her baby would be a boy or a girl; I said I didn't like to forecast such things and she must wait and be thankful for what she is given."

"And that's what you want to say to me?" Emma asked drily. "All right, I can wait. I don't care what it is if it's healthy and has the right number of fingers and toes."

"There will be the right number," Emily said quietly. "Just rest well and come to see me soon. See Stella and leave the housekeeping to Eileen."

"You will be here when it comes?" Emma felt a pang of apprehension.

"If you need me, but that's a long way off."

"I'll need you," Emma said softly. "I'll always need you."

"You have your own strength, but I'll be there," Emily promised. She chuckled. "Look out those maternity clothes and tell me if you want anything. Let me know what Stella says."

Fourteen

"It was nice to get out with Mick," Eileen said. Mick grinned and eyed his wife with tolerant humour. "She managed to forget Jean for two hours," he said, "and even suggested that we stop to buy fish and chips on the way home, like we used to do."

Emma laughed. "And when you got back, Jean was still alive and fast asleep."

Eileen busied herself in the kitchen with more energy than she'd shown since Jean had contracted chickenpox. "It was a lovely evening. We saw the news too and a bit about the Eurovision Song Contest they had some time ago. They said they might have it every year, with lots of countries taking part, but I couldn't understand a word the singer said. Where's Lugano?"

"Switzerland," Paul said. "Is that where they had it?"

"A girl called Lys Assid won with a song called 'Refrain'. Let's hope a British singer wins next time," Mick said. "I thought it a bit soppy but Eileen liked the clothes everyone wore. Some were a bit . . . you know . . . and I don't want you wearing anything like it," he said sternly. "Some of them showed more than you'd see in an underwear advert."

"And you didn't enjoy that, I suppose?" Eileen said.

"Not on my wife," Mick said. "They showed a lot about show business. I liked the bit about Elvis Presley. Now there's a *real* singer." Mick danced a few steps and intoned the only words he knew from the song. "You can do most anything but don't tread on my blue suede shoes."

"If I can't have pretty clothes like the film stars, you can't have suede shoes," Eileen said. "Do you know, I caught him looking at a pair in that shop down the road? Mrs Coster says that only pimps and swindlers wear them, so you can polish up your old brown brogues or buy some soft slip-ons."

"They were plain brown," Mick protested. "I think they're very smart."

Emma and Paul left them happily wrangling and went into the consulting room. Rose was in her bedroom doing a puzzle that Emma had found in the collection of toys they had bought in Ireland and Jean was dressing her dolls. She was quiet and less demanding now, and her spots were fading, but she wasn't allowed out of her own home until there was no possibility of her passing on any infection to Paul's patients.

"I think the evening out did a lot for them," Paul remarked. He grinned. "Mick seems to have had more than fish and chips when he got home. He hasn't had that light in his eyes for some time."

Emma laughed. "Whatever it was, Eileen looks happier and she has decided that Jean can't have everything she wants and have her dancing attendance all the time."

"*You* convinced her of that: Jean takes notice of what you say," Paul remarked. "By the way, I organised a session with Stella this afternoon, so be ready at two and I'll drive you there."

"I can manage it alone," Emma began.

"I'll take you. This concerns me too, and I shall take you to have tea afterwards if it's good news."

"What if it isn't?"

"It will be, but if it isn't, I'll still take you to tea at the Ritz."

"Aren't you forgetting something?"

"I can forget patients. Robert will take over."

"Not that. A full cream tea would be wasted. I shall have Marmite sandwiches and an apple for lunch, and possibly a boiled egg for dinner."

"What do I have? *I'm* not pregnant!"

"You won't starve," Emma said unsympathetically. "I think you have a patient now. I hear Mrs Coster in her royal mode showing someone upstairs. We should have bought more than one really pretty apron. She's wearing that one to death."

"Ask Bea to send another. I take it you'll be phoning her today?"

"Whatever the news." She smiled. "Aunt Emily saw no hitches and wants me to take Rose there for a day or so. It's a bit soon to be going there again, but I think it's a good idea."

"I do, too. Now, work," he said softly. "Good morning, Mrs Mortimer."

Emma took her jacket and settled her comfortably on the couch. Mrs Mortimer sighed. "I feel better just coming into this room." Her scars were fading but her hand was held awkwardly and seemed to have lost its function. Emma touched it and the skin was cold.

"How has it been?" Paul asked. He consulted her notes. "It's two months since the car accident, but Dr Forsyth wanted me to see you. He says you look a lot better than when you came here first but I am the one who uses hypnosis, and that may ease your mind about what happened. Do you use that hand yet?"

She shook her head but said nothing. Paul looked at the notes again. "Sister, will you ask Mr Grade to take over from you? I want him to make notes."

Emma looked surprised but left the room and asked Mick to take over.

"I expect you're busy," he assumed. "Straightforward hypnosis, is it?"

"Paul has the Thiopentone and there's everything he might need. Call me when she's ready to get off the couch and I'll bring her a cup of tea."

She was puzzled. The housekeeping was under control and the two girls were playing happily, so there was no need for Paul to send her away from what seemed like a routine consultation.

Robert put this head round the kitchen door. "Is Mrs Mortimer in there?" he asked. "I thought she must have gone, as you aren't with Paul."

"I was dismissed," Emma said shortly.

"Maybe I'll look in," he said. "Paul must have thought you had other things to do."

After half an hour of mixing a cake that they didn't

really need, Emma put it in the oven and read the daily paper, feeling unwanted.

At last Mick came out of the consulting room. "She's all yours, sister. If there's tea going, Himself can do with a cup, too." He shook his head. "Shocking business."

Emma made tea and carried the tray into the consulting room. She helped Mrs Mortimer into her jacket and shoes and poured tea. Paul looked tense, as if the session had drained him, but the patient was relaxed and drank her tea eagerly. Emma noticed that the hand that had been so limp was now able to hold a cup.

"Why did you push me out?" Emma asked as soon as Mrs Mortimer had left.

Paul eyed her with caution. "I didn't want you to hear what she'd say under hypnosis."

"She didn't seem all that ill, and her scars had faded almost completely – or so Robert said."

"She had malfunction of one hand that didn't respond to physio," Paul said.

"I noticed it was better when she took her cup," Emma recalled.

Paul sat down and took a deep breath. "The examination wasn't as bad as I thought, but even so, you would have found it traumatic just now. When the car crashed she was in the passenger seat with a baby who was wearing no restraint, although Mrs Mortimer was wearing a seatbelt. The baby was thrown out of her control and her hand was trapped when she tried to clutch the child."

"So she felt it was her fault that the baby was hurt?"

"Yes. Fortunately no real harm was done and the

child is fine, but each night Mrs Mortimer dreams that the child died; and the hand that failed to hold the baby refuses to work, or it did until today. She will need further analysis but she'll be well soon," he added with a reassuring smile.

"I'm glad to hear about it after your session and not while I was there," Emma admitted. "Thank you, Paul. I'm not really ready to face an account of harm to a baby. You know me too well, but it couldn't have been easy for you either, now that there may be a baby for us on the way."

"Well, this afternoon Stella can make sure that we're right," Paul said cheerfully. "We can eat at Mario's tonight and you can have plain spaghetti while I have a decent meal."

"I may be hungry and eat more than you do," she said.

He kissed her. "Be as difficult as you like. I still love you."

A jacket that Emma had discarded months ago as being too loose now seemed the perfect comfortable garment to wear when she saw Stella, and a long loose shirt and baggy trousers completed the picture of easy acceptance of the fact that she was not quite as lissom as usual.

Paul smiled and said nothing, but drove carefully as if the car contained a precious box of cut glass.

"I hoped I'd see you soon," Stella said as soon as Emma was sitting by the examination couch and had removed her jacket. She made a few notes and cast a practised gaze over Emma's figure and breasts. She took a blood-pressure reading and counted her pulse. "Fine," she said and chewed the end of her pen.

"You sounded surprised," Emma remarked.

"Not really. I saw that you're healthy as soon as you came in here, but you seem further on than I thought possible from your dates. Hop on the scales. I have a note of what you weighed the last time you came here for an examination, so let's compare. You've put on weight, I think."

"Too much good Irish food," Emma suggested.

"Maybe." Stella sounded pensive and checked the reading on the scales a second time. "No swollen ankles, and your specimen is clear, and you think you are two months pregnant."

"Perhaps three months," Emma said.

"On the couch." Stella felt the rising fundus of the uterus just behind the rigid pubic bone and smiled. "Three months, I think."

"I've had no sickness," Emma said as if she disbelieved Stella's words.

"Aren't you the lucky one! You may escape that and just bloom happily. It must have been the Guinness or the seafood!"

"Why is it so amusing? Are you sure everything's all right?"

"I don't need to do an internal today. It's quite, quite positive without me interfering at this stage."

"You're sure?"

"Sure and doubly sure." Stella gave a delighted laugh. "As far as I can tell, and I'm pretty sure even now, I think you may have twins in there."

170

"I can't believe it!" Tears of shock rolled down Emma's cheeks but she felt calm and happy. She began to giggle. "Bea will be thrilled. She'll say that I try to outdo her even now, and pretend to be jealous, then probably make an excuse to come over to see for herself how I am."

Stella wagged an admonishing finger at her. "You will now vegetate and do exactly as you are told."

"Yes, ma'am," Emma said humbly. "May I go now and tell Paul?"

"I suppose that aunt of yours knows?"

"How can she? Oh, dear, she does! When I said I didn't mind what it was so long as it was healthy and had all its fingers and toes, she said something about there being the right number of everything."

"Twenty tiny fingers and twenty tiny toes . . . as the song says. I could use her in the clinic."

"She's promised to be here when it happens and she doesn't seem worried," Emma said slowly. "I don't know why I feel so calm, but I trust her almost as much as I trust you. I know I shall be fine."

"I'm proud to be included with your diagnosing aunt," Stella said, and laughed. "Make sure you rest and eat sensibly and have lots of friends visiting you – if you don't have to work hard entertaining them – and see me in two weeks' time."

Paul was waiting by the desk in reception, talking to an old friend who was still working at Beattie's as an anaesthetist. The two men stopped talking and eyed Emma with speculation. "Well?" asked Paul.

"Very well," Stella said. "Emma, meet Martin and

171

smile at him. We might need an anaesthetist who can help you without making you sick. No, don't be alarmed, Paul. Just looking ahead at all contingencies. Some women *do* have a caesarean for twins, but I doubt if Emma will need that." She chuckled. "Ask her Aunt Emily and let me know what to expect."

"Twins?" For a moment Paul completely lost his calm and held Emma's hands in his. "Really twins?"

"I don't think it's more than two," Stella said. "Come into my sitting room and have coffee before you drive anywhere, Paul. It's quite a shock, isn't it?"

She showed them where her room was and asked the ward maid to take in coffee, then pleaded pressure of work and left them alone.

"It's wonderful," Paul said with a note of awe.

Emma said shakily, "I feel rather like a brood mare, and Stella wants me to become a calm fat cow!"

"Not both," he said in mock alarm. "But you will have to take everything slowly and rest a lot. No alarming tales from the clinic, and Maureen will have to look after Rose."

"Paul! This is *me*. I am fit and must have exercise as well as rest and Rose is very good now, so please don't smother me with care, much as I enjoy it," she said and kissed him. "No coffee for me, just water from that jug, and I must buy some fruit juice. What I'd like now is a mint humbug and a banana."

"Not at the same time?"

"Possibly," she replied, teasing him. "You look terrible, darling. I'll ask Robert to have you in for a session to iron out your hang-ups and anxieties. Ready? I have

letters to write and calls to make. Can't waste time
here." It was as if a niggling veil was lifted away,
revealing the blue sky again, and she was full of
excited energy.

"Do we tell her?" Paul asked when they opened the front
door and met Mrs Coster, who was wiping her hands on
her scrubbing-apron.

"How can we avoid it? She's lying in wait for
the news."

"What did she tell you that we didn't know already?"
Mrs Coster asked in a superior voice. "I've had enough
babies, I ought to know. I said to Maureen I thought
you'd got your dates wrong. That jacket will soon be
too tight."

"I know," Emma said. "We did get one thing wrong.
I might have twins."

"Just wait until I tell Maureen! You'll really need a
full-time nanny when they come," she announced with
satisfaction. Mrs Coster dried her hands and picked up
her bucket. "You're healthy so it should be as easy as
shelling peas from a pod," she said.

"First I'm a brood mare and now I'm a pea pod,"
Emma whispered. "What next, when I tell Bea? But
first there's Eileen and Mick, otherwise Mrs Coster will
tell them and they'll be hurt."

"Why not post a bulletin in the hall and let the whole
of Kensington into the secret?" Paul said drily. "Oh,
here's Robert; I think I can just beat Mrs Coster to it. See
you at lunch, if we're eating. You'd better get to Eileen
now. Mrs Coster has *important news* in her eyes."

"Rose has to know," Emma said, biting her lip. "How will she react?"

"I'll tell her that when you saw the children in Ireland you thought it would be a good idea to have a baby brother or sister for her to play with and look after. I don't think it's a good idea to say the leprechauns gave you a wish, or she might wish too hard and we'll find ourselves with quads!"

"Are you going to be faddy over food?" was Eileen's first reaction. She seemed on edge, and when Emma added that she was not only pregnant but it might be twins, Eileen burst into tears. "It's not fair," she sobbed.

"I thought you didn't want another baby."

"I don't know. Sometimes I do, and then I think of being fat again and hate the idea. Jean wants a sister and Mick keeps on about us having another and now he'll be mad at me for not copying you."

"If it's important to either of you there's plenty of time," Emma suggested.

"I like my job and I like being slim again," Eileen said with a toss of her head. "I didn't have much before I married Mick and now I feel . . . important." She blushed. "The butcher down the road calls me madam and the postman acts as if I'm mistress of the house. It may not be much to you, but it is to me."

Emma smiled. "You are mistress of the household. A skilled housekeeper rules her own little kingdom and you look after us very well."

"That's nice to know," Eileen said. "What do you want for lunch?"

"The same as Paul and Robert. It's soup and sandwiches today, isn't it?"

Mick looked bleak when he met her, then turned away at the office door. Emma wondered what he thought about the news, and when Eileen brought the soup into the dining room she noticed that she had a very red face and had been crying. She piled rolls on to a dish and made sure there were plates for the sandwiches and cheese.

Emma noticed that Paul had seen the tears too but neither of them mentioned it to Eileen or Mick.

A crash from the kitchen and a muffled expletive told them that Mick was not his usual calm self and was very annoyed.

"And our next patient will be . . ." whispered Robert.

"It could happen when Nuala and Liam come to stay," Paul said. "Mick has always wanted a boy and Liam is such a little tough guy he'd fit into his scheme of what a son should be and bring Mick a lot of joy."

"They do say that pregnancy is catching," Emma reminded them. "Perhaps this will happen to them and everyone will be happy. I can't bear to see such good people upset."

Paul saw her yawn. "You have to have a nap each afternoon," he told her. "Stella was firm about that."

Emma tried to look stubborn. "Doesn't the brood mare have an opinion?"

"No," both men said together.

She sighed and picked up her jacket. "See you later. I ought to look at my wardrobe again. I feel a bit bloated and I can't think of much that will fit me in a few weeks' time."

"Joan will help you," Robert assured her. Emma looked at the two men and smiled. It was wonderful to have such care.

"I'll leave it until she comes here," she said. "At least I shall be fine for your wedding," she added, and gave them a look that forbade any disagreement. "Nothing has changed. I have the reception all planned and Maureen is coming in for a whole day to help with the children."

Mick was loitering outside the kitchen when she went out to go to her room. He grinned apologetically. "I haven't said congratulations."

"No need, Mick. We both know how you feel about us and I know that you will have another baby one day, so don't be too hurt that Eileen wants a breathing space."

He looked ashamed. "I went spare when the doc told me, and took it out on her. First time I've made her cry for ages."

"I think Eileen realises that Jean needs a brother or a sister, so go carefully and don't make her stubborn just for the sake of paying you out." Her dimples appeared mischievously. "Say you're sorry you were upset but that you were disappointed for her, as it's not fair that we should have all the fun and she would feel left out!"

Mick laughed. "Too many shrinks round here, but I see what you mean. I'll be as nice as pie and once Jean starts whining that she wants a baby too, I think that will settle that old lark."

Fifteen

"Have you something I can take with me to read?" Margaret looked along the bookshelves and picked out a light novel, then put it back. "I've gone off romantic novels and I'm not up to more serious books since Alistair was born. I think he fancies himself as a tub-thumper. He makes enough very determined noise for a Member of Parliament!"

"Wind," Emma said firmly.

"Too much spoiling," replied Margaret. "Janey can't resist him and picks him up as soon as he starts whimpering."

"Does it bother you?" Emma shifted into a more comfortable position in the deep armchair and winced when her sciatic nerve pointed out that a couple of babies was a burden that wasn't natural, especially when they kicked.

"Not at all, I love it, but coming to London was a very good idea. George will be off his ship today and we can go home together after he's been debriefed at the Admiralty. He can hold his son when he bawls and I can look on indulgently."

"You look very happy."

"I'm so happy I could burst, and I want to make George happy too."

"You've already done that, and he'll come back to a slim and beautiful wife with a baby boy who looks like him." Emma smoothed her heavy lump and sighed. "You give me courage. It *will* be over and I *might* get my figure back."

"Aunt Emily said she'll be with you in a day or so and stay for a while." Margaret laughed. "She's such a wonderful person. She told me that Alistair would be delivered quickly and without fuss and he was. He couldn't wait to get into the world and fight for his place in it!"

"Clive seems pleased."

"He sees another sailor coming into the family. And he's so busy at school that he hasn't really had time to be jealous."

"Paul is taking you to the Admiralty to pick up George, and the powers that be will take you to Hampshire, so I shan't see you or George again this time." She laughed. "In fact, I shall be having a nap, as befits a wallowing whale!"

"She's got over the brood-mare stage," Paul said. He grinned. "I wouldn't dare call her a whale but I do see her point."

"I almost wish I knew what to expect," Emma said with a frown. "Maybe it's as well that I can't even guess, but two of the same sex might be nice, or then one of each might be even better."

"Whatever they are will be welcome," Paul said warmly.

Emma and the Leprechauns

"At least I can't complain of the care I'm having," Emma said. "Bea was here last week and brought a lot of lovely baby things, plus her own brand of caustic humour which put me in my place when I moaned about my lump and did a lot of good. She has a lot in common with Aunt Emily and sneaked off to see her for a day, to Emily's delight."

"What about your friends in Ireland?"

Emma sighed. "They couldn't come because Patrick fell off a horse and spent a week in hospital, but they will come later."

"Why are you laughing?" Margaret asked.

"You haven't asked about the help I have *here*."

"Why? Is there a problem?"

"Eileen has watched with ill-concealed horror as my girth extended rapidly and remembers when she was carrying Jean."

"Has it put her off having another?"

"Too late!"

"What do you mean?"

"I don't know what went on downstairs, but Eileen was very cross for a week or so recently, as if she'd been made to do something she wanted to avoid."

Margaret giggled. "You think Mick had his evil unprotected way with her?"

"It would be more polite to say he exerted his lawful conjugal rights," Paul said.

"And has anything happened?"

"Nothing, apart from morning sickness," Emma said with an innocent air. "I shall have to spoil her a little as soon as I've got over this. I didn't show her the baby clothes that Bea brought over, but some will go to Eileen. Most of the girls' things are very pretty and I hope she has a girl as she doesn't care for boys."

"For the first few months it doesn't matter if a boy wears skirts. It's easier to keep clean."

"Is that the reason? In Ireland they say that all babies should wear girls' clothes for the first two years or so in case the leprechauns steal the boy babies."

"You don't believe that?"

"Of course not – and Aunt Emily is a match for any old leprechaun – but I'm glad we didn't give the girls the dolls we brought back from Ireland. It might give Eileen ideas!"

"Alistair is yelling his little head off," Mick said complacently from the doorway. "What a lovely sound."

"I'll remind you of that remark very soon, Mick, and when ours are a bit more civilised, it will be your turn."

Mick blushed. "You heard Eileen in the loo?"

"Several times, so there can be no mistake. Have you taken her for a check?"

"Today. She has come to terms with it now, and is better than I thought possible."

"As soon as you tell us the news officially, I have some clothes she might like. I kept that rather nice silk suit that I wore during the early part of my pregnancy. She admired it so she can wear that."

"And I suggest that, as soon as she's eating more, you take her to Mario's in her best clothes for a celebration meal. That will do a lot for her morale. Mario has this fixation with pregnant women and thinks they are all beautiful and precious! He'll kiss her hand and make you jealous and she'll love it, as Emma did," Paul added drily.

Mick laughed. "Know what, doc? You'd make a good shrink!"

Margaret came back carrying her son. "A nice full nappy," she said happily. "With any luck he won't do it when George first sees him. "Shall we go now?"

She kissed Emma and held her tenderly. "I'll be with you in spirit, and Emily will tell me what is happening."

Paul packed the car with the bundles of nappies and other paraphernalia that small babies acquire, and Emma waved goodbye from a window.

She turned away and tried to read the newspaper but she was restless. Paul was busy with a patient and Robert was away for the day sorting out the flat in Covent Garden which was still convenient for him and his wife when they were in the West End or when Joan was working in casualty after their brief honeymoon.

Emma heaved her bulk out of the chair and went into the kitchen. She strained the chicken broth and added parsley and potato-flour thickener, making enough for Eileen, Mick and Jean as well as her own family and checking that there was enough bread for toast to go with it. Rose was helping Mrs Coster turn out a cupboard that gave up several lost toys and a few cobwebs, and Jean was playing with a friend in the basement.

Eileen sniffed and smiled. "I was coming to do that, sister. It does smell good. I'll take Jean's friend home and call Mick as we have to go out this afternoon."

"It's good to see you hungry again," Emma said. "I heard you being sick a few times and asked Mick about it. He said you're going for a check today, so come back and tell me all about it. I'll lay the kitchen table and we can eat together."

Eileen came back after taking the little girl home and tidying Jean. Mrs Coster brushed Rose's hair and washed her hands, promising to wipe the dust from the long-lost toys before they went up to the nursery.

"The dolls can go to Jean," Rose said. "I'll keep the puzzles and the books."

"What if your mummy has a baby girl? You'll need dolls for her."

Rose shrugged. "She'll be like me and want a donkey," she replied. "And the boy will be like Mark and Liam and want a donkey too."

"It may be two girls," Emma said from the top of the stairs.

Rose wrinkled her nose. "No, I asked the leppercorns to send one of each."

"They can't do that. They are only fairy creatures."

"They like me," Rose said. "When I was down with Aunt Emily, I had a dream and they were very nice."

Emma took her into the kitchen where Paul was waiting for lunch. "Tell Daddy about it while I get the soup," she said with a warning glance at Paul.

Rose looked stubborn. "You told me there are no leppercorns but I saw them in my dream at Aunt Emily's and I talked to them and they told me about the babies."

182

"What if they were wrong, Rose?"

"They tell the truth."

"Not all the time," Paul said.

Rose darted away to fetch a book that Emma had overlooked when she wanted to remove anything about leprechauns and she showed them a picture of a leprechaun peeping round a large milk jug in a kitchen. "See!" Rose said triumphantly. "There are some."

"I didn't see it when I looked at that book."

Rose giggled. "The ones in my dream said he hid until you closed the book and then came out again."

"They may be wrong about the babies," Emma said again.

Rose took the book away and Paul said softly, "I'd be more worried if they were right. Do we have another Emily in the family?"

Mick answered the phone and called Emma. "It's your aunt," he said.

"Aunt Emily?"

"Just to say I shall be with you tomorrow, if that's all right? My doctor friend has to go to London and Surrey and said he'll bring me to you before he goes off to Reigate."

"That's wonderful. Tell him to be here for lunch," Emma said.

She walked back to the kitchen feeling pensive. Emily had mentioned that she might have to hire a car to bring her to London as the doctor would be unavailable in two weeks' time and she didn't want to have to twiddle her thumbs waiting for the birth for several days before it was due. She shrugged. Maybe

Emily was ready for a holiday and wanted to come early after all.

Emma put the remains of the chicken soup in a jug for Eileen to use and made a large Cornish pasty for lunch the next day. Stewed fruit would be enough for pudding, and she had ordered bread from the shop down the road. She went to sleep on the bed and woke feeling energetic enough to check over the case containing the clothes and toilet things that she'd want in the private wing of Beattie's when she needed to be admitted. She smiled. Silly me, she thought. I have another two weeks to wait, so nothing is urgent.

Rose came into the bedroom and sat on the bed. "Daddy said he'd help me write a letter to Liam when the babies have come." She leaned across nearer to Emma and put a hand on the swollen abdomen. She squealed with laughter. "That boy kicked me," she said.

"Not the girl?"

"She doesn't kick as hard," Rose said calmly. "See you soon," she said as she left the room; once again Emma felt that Emily was close.

Paul brought her hot lemon and a biscuit and drank his tea with her in the bedroom. "Everything all right?" he asked.

"I think so, but it will happen earlier than I imagined. Emily wouldn't come here before she had to, and even Rose seems to expect something soon."

"Shall I ring Stella and tell her your psychic aunt is on her way here, so clear the decks for action?"

"Of course not. She'd think we were crazy. You don't

think we are, do you? I haven't even a twinge. By the way, I've baked a pasty while you were out, for Emily and Dr Sutton tomorrow."

Paul could almost hear Stella's voice: "Let her do what she can and don't try to make her rest when she doesn't need it. She's strong and healthy but as soon as she gets restless and starts to make a nest – looking ahead and baking, tidying drawers and seeming to expect something to happen – ring me and we'll have her in before she goes into labour. Twins can make a few problems that can be avoided if we keep an eye on her."

He closed the door to the office while he called Beattie's.

"I was about to ring you," Stella said. "Emma has two more weeks to go but I would like her here tomorrow. A pity her aunt isn't coming to you until the dates we suggested, but never mind."

"When my wife does as you said, works to get everything ready, and then Emily announces that she's coming here tomorrow, two weeks early, I thought it was time I rang you," he said and laughed.

"Bring her in tomorrow afternoon," Stella said. "I never argue with witches. We may induce or it may be a caesarean."

"I brought you some rabbits from the farm," Emily said as soon as she'd said hello and asked if Emma was all right. "I'll cook them, as Eileen may be squeamish just now."

Paul grinned and kissed her cheek. "You bring an

equal quantity of sanity and madness to this house, and I know that everything will be fine."

"Did you doubt it?" Her eyes were full of the tenderness she hardly ever showed in physical contact, but she allowed Paul to hug her. "Janey sends her love," she said brusquely. "I'd better see Emma now if you'll take my bag up."

"Lunch as soon as Dr Sutton's ready, and a nice cup of tea afterwards," Paul said with a grin.

"Aunt Emily!" Emma and Rose converged on her and Rose clung to her coat.

"Are you staying to look after me while Mummy is away?"

"I thought you were going to look after *me*," Emily said. "I dare say we'll get on." She looked at Emma. "So you're going in today." She seemed pleased. "I did wonder."

"It's too early, but Stella is a bit fussy over twins."

"I told her you'd be here," Paul said. "That made up her mind to admit Emma now."

Emily looked embarrassed. "Nothing to do with me."

"It's going to be one of each, Aunt Emily."

"Is it, Rose? We'll wait and see." But she eyed the child with slight concern and changed the subject.

"If we are going, I'd rather be there or I'll need a nap," Emma said later. Paul took her case and extra jacket and a packet of fruit sweets, and Rose and Emily waved them off in the car.

"I'll ring this evening to say good-night," Paul said as soon as Emma was shown into her comfortable room.

"Yes, darling, do that," Emma said as if indulging a child.

Paul left, feeling excluded from the ancient feminine rites of new life, and Emma almost forgot her family for a while.

"A lot of hard work, but I think you can manage, Emma," Stella said. "I'll induce now and see what happens."

The injection to dilate the opening to the womb made Emma sleepy. She woke feeling as if she had a bad stomachache, then slept again until it was worse and Stella was examining her.

"Good girl. You can push gently now."

Emma tried to concentrate through the clouds of gas and air but was glad to leave everything to skilful hands. She heard a short laugh from the nurse giving her gas and air and felt the slippery baby released over her abdomen, then a pause. More gas and air gave her respite during the next contractions and she was suddenly free.

A nurse wiped her wet brow and Stella smiled her satisfaction over the white mask. "One of each, you clever girl," she said. "No stitches and everything complete including fingers and toes. We'll clean you up and then you must sleep. You'll see the babies soon but they need a bath, too."

Sleep came deeply and covered her mind. The muted sounds of clearing up the room and the small sounds of babies crying didn't disturb her until dawn. Her abdomen was flat but soggy and her body felt light as air. "Is it all over?" she asked in wonder.

187

"All over," said Paul. "Or all beginning," he added and yawned, but his happiness glowed through the exhaustion of a sleepless night.

"Go to bed," she told him. "I want to see them and then I shall have another nap."

"I'll bring the family this evening," he said. "Stella will let you see the twins later and said you must rest."

"Are they all right?"

"They're gorgeous! Now go back to sleep."

Emily put her head round the door and laughed. "We came just for five minutes," she said. "But I must say you look fine, just fine."

"Is Rose there?"

"She's being shown the babies and is coming with Paul."

"Mummy, they are small!" Rose tried to be calm.

"Not small for babies," Emma said.

"I said we'd have one of each," Rose said proudly.

"So you did," said Emily and eyed her great-niece with a quizzical gaze. "So you did."

"Five more minutes," the nurse said. "Have you everything you want, Mrs Sykes?"

Emma looked at the loving eager faces round her. "I have everything I shall ever want. My family is complete," she said.